Copyright © 2021 by Loi

All rights reserved. No part of this text may be reproduced, transmitted, downloaded, decompiled, reverse-engineered, or stored in, or introduced into any information storage and retrieval system, in any form or by any means, whether electronic or mechanical, now known, hereinafter invented, without express written permission of the publisher. For permission requests, write to the publisher, addressed "Attention: Permissions Coordinator," at the address below.

Typewriter Pub, an imprint of Blvnp Incorporated
A Nevada Corporation
1887 Whitney Mesa DR #2002
Henderson, NV 89014
www.typewriterpub.com/info@typewriterpub.com

ISBN: 978-1-64434-153-7

DISCLAIMER
This book is a work of fiction. The characters, incidents, and dialogue are drawn from the author's imagination and are not to be construed as real. While references might be made to actual historical events or existing locations, the names, characters, places, and incidents are either products of the author's imagination or are used fictitiously, and any resemblance to actual persons living or dead, business establishments, events or locales is entirely coincidental.

LUNA
The First 30 Days
BOOK TWO

LORA POWELL

For Gram.
I miss you every day.
Thank you for always believing in me.

CHAPTER ONE

Day One

Mommy wasn't feeling good. I could tell because she gave me a bowl of cereal for breakfast. She knew I hated cereal. She almost never served me the stuff. Instead, she made me pancakes with chocolate chips every morning. The only times the dreaded box of little round O's appeared was when she had a stuffy nose. Or had been coughing. Or something.

I pushed the soggy mess around in the milk with my spoon. I hoped lunch turned out better than breakfast because I was not eating this. The spoon clattered to the bowl when I dropped it.

Mommy jumped at the sound. Holding her hand to her head, she turned around from where she had been washing dishes at the sink.

"I'm sorry, kiddo. Mommy's not feeling very well this morning. I know you don't like cereal."

Mommy didn't look very good. Her face was all red, and her mouth was pinched together like Mrs. Green's did when she was really unhappy about something. Mommy never made the unhappy teacher face; her mouth always smiled and laughed. Suddenly, I felt bad that I didn't eat the cereal.

My sneakers slapped the floor when I dropped down from the bar stool. Going around the bar, I grabbed Mommy and hugged her. I always felt better when she kissed an ouchie, so I figured the same was probably true the other way around. Grabbing her hand, I kissed the palm of it loudly.

"Thanks, kid." She ruffled her hand through my hair, her fingers getting caught on a little knot. My hair was always getting knots. I hated when Mommy brushed it. It pulled no matter how gentle she tried to be. "Let's get you ready for school, the bus will be here soon."

I hurried to grab Mr. Cuddles from where he had been watching me not eat my breakfast on the bar. Mr. Cuddles was missing some of his fur and Mommy replaced his lost nose with a button, but he was still my best toy in the whole world. He hid in my purple pony backpack every day when I went to school. I didn't care what Mrs. Green said, I didn't go anywhere without Mr. Cuddles.

Mommy's hands felt really warm when they touched my skin. She put my hair up in a ponytail with my favorite green hair tie and checked that my shoes were double knotted. I still couldn't tie them myself, but I didn't want my friends at school to know, so she tied them extra good in the morning, that way they would stay all day.

It was only the second week of school, but I was already ready for it to be over. Last year, I only had to go for a little while in the morning, then I had gotten to go to the daycare for lunch and to play with my friends until Mommy got done at work. This year, I had to stay at school all day.

Mrs. Green wasn't as fun as Miss Mallory at the daycare had been. Mrs. Green made the unhappy squished face a lot.

Mommy walked with me to the bus stop every morning. The steps down from our door weren't slippery, so I didn't know why Mommy slipped. She caught herself on the railing and flashed me a smile that didn't make me feel any better.

"It's okay. I'm going to walk you to the bus, then Mommy's going to go home and take a nap."

Mommy *never* didn't go to work. She said that if she didn't work, the lights wouldn't turn on when we flicked the switch. The other kids at school all said that their mommies and daddies worked too, so that 'light' thing must be normal. I didn't have a daddy. I figured that meant that my mommy had to work even harder, so hearing Mommy say that she was going to nap instead of going to work made me worried.

I liked where we lived because our house was so close to other houses that had other kids. There was always lots of them around to play with. A couple of other mommies were walking their kids to the bus too. Bigger kids walked themselves in groups, dragging their feet in the stones because they didn't want to go to school either.

All the little roads that went between the rows of houses turned into a bigger road with a stop sign. Next to that stop sign was where we waited for the bus. I held on to Mommy's sweaty hand. Normally, she talked to me while we waited, but today, she was quiet.

The big yellow bus came, and everyone began to climb on. I gave Mommy a hug around her waist and she squeezed my shoulders.

"I'll see you after school. Love you, baby."

"Bye, Mommy. I love you too." I let go of her and climbed onto the bus. My seat was on the same side of the bus where Mommy stood, which made me happy because I got to wave at her one last time as the bus drove away.

We had assigned seats, and I normally had to sit with a girl who was older than me. I didn't like her very much. She made fun of my red hair. I thought my hair was okay; it looked a lot like Mommy's, so I didn't know why she didn't like it. Mommy's hair was pretty.

She wasn't on the bus today, so that made me happy too. Now that I thought about it, there were a lot of empty seats today. There must have been a lot of people who were sick like Mommy.

The school looked normal when we pulled up to the front doors. Other kids were getting off other buses. Someone was putting the flag up on the flagpole. The policeman that watched us go into the building every morning was standing in the same spot that he always did. The steps on the bus were really high, and I always had a hard time going down them, especially when bigger kids behind me wanted me to hurry up.

The hallway inside the school was colorful and loud with so many people trying to talk to each other at once. Mrs. Green's room was all the way at the end of the hall. Hanging on to my backpack, I trudged towards the door. When I got there, I was startled by Mrs. Green standing by the doorway.

"Luna, here." The teacher waved a big bottle of hand sanitizer at me. "Rub some of this all over your hands. There's a bad flu going around, and I don't want it getting into my classroom." She squirted a blob of the runny gel on to my palm.

I wrinkled my nose but did as she told me. Arguing with the teacher didn't work, I already tried, and it just made Mommy upset when the teacher called her.

At the back of the room near my cubby, I zipped open my backpack and peeked in at Mr. Cuddles. He looked comfy enough sitting at the bottom of the bag, so I zipped it back up and stuffed the bag in the spot marked with my name. Jaime threw her own backpack into the next cubby, still rubbing the slimy hand sanitizer from Mrs. Green on to her skin.

"Hi, Jaime."

"Hi, Luna. Mrs. Green's being even weirder than normal."

"Yeah," I agreed as we walked to our desks. Jaime was my best friend and we sat next to each other. Mrs. Green must not have known because I was sure she wouldn't have let us sit together if she did.

We watched as the teacher made every kid who came in the room use the hand sanitizer. When the bell finally rang, she closed the door with a bang and vigorously rubbed several squirts of the stuff all over her own hands and arms. I rolled my eyes at Jaime so she would know what I thought of Mrs. Green.

Jaime sat to my left. There was usually a boy named Jake to my right, but his seat was empty. Looking around, I noticed that it looked like there were as many empty seats as ones with kids in them. Maybe Mrs. Green wasn't totally wrong about that flu after all.

CHAPTER TWO

Day Two

My stomach was growling by the time Mrs. Green told us to get our snack. I tore open my backpack eagerly to search for the little plastic bag of fish-shaped crackers that I knew Mommy had packed for me today. Those crackers were my favorite thing out of all the choices that she sent for my snack.

I was so excited to get those crackers that I forgot to open my backpack just far enough to reach inside. Mr. Cuddles spilled out onto the floor at my feet.

Before I could grab him, someone hurried by, kicking Mr. Cuddles. I watched as my bear skidded halfway across the room and came to a stop at Mrs. Green's feet.

She bent down and picked him up by one ear. "Who does this belong to?" Her face scrunched up and she glared down her nose.

"That's my Mr. Cuddles." I stepped forward with the bag of crackers clutched in my hands. I didn't look away from my bear. I needed to get him back.

"Luna, you know that you aren't to have toys at school."

"I know but—"

She cut me off, turning abruptly to stalk to her desk. "You may have it back at the end of the day. If you bring a toy to school again, I'm going to have to call your mom." She opened the big drawer at the bottom of her desk and dropped Mr. Cuddles inside. She closed the drawer.

I stood where I was, looking at the place where Mr. Cuddles disappeared until she snapped at me to sit down. I plopped on to my seat and grudgingly began eating my snack, wishing with all my strength that Mrs. Green's head would explode. It wasn't fair. Mr. Cuddles stayed in my backpack all day. I didn't play with him at school.

There was some sort of commotion in the hall as we were finishing our snacks. The teacher cracked the door to look out, then slammed it again. She looked kinda pale when she turned back around. Muttering under her breath that she was glad she was not the janitor, she went to her desk and pumped more of that hand sanitizer on to her palm.

We were practicing to write numbers one through ten when the principal made a sudden announcement over the loudspeaker.

"All students and staff are to remain indoors until further notice. Staff should keep their room doors closed. Any person showing signs of illness should report to the nurse's office immediately."

I couldn't remember the principal ever making an announcement like that before. School was usually easy for me, but between the strange announcement and Mr. Cuddles being held hostage in Mrs. Green's desk, I was having a hard time concentrating on what I was supposed to be doing. It seemed like hours dragged by before it was time to go eat lunch.

There was a big wet spot on the floor when we left our classroom. One of those yellow signs with the funny drawing of a man slipping was propped nearby. Mrs. Green made sure that none of us stepped in the wet spot as we filed out of the room.

The cafeteria was way up by the front doors. Our class was always last to get there, and the room was noisy and crowded. Except it was a little less noisy and a lot less crowded than usual. Jaime and I got in line to buy our food.

"She better give you Mr. Cuddles back."

Jaime was just as mad at our teacher as I was over her putting my bear in her desk. That was why she and I were best friends. Jaime wasn't annoying like a lot of the other girls in our class. I always knew what her opinion was going to be about everything.

It was nacho day at school. I took a tray and pressed the buttons on the pin pad that Mommy made me memorize for the first day of school. Paying for my lunch that way always made me smile. It made me feel grown up like how Mommy pushed buttons on a pin pad to pay at the grocery store.

I carried my tray to our class table. Jaime was already stuffing nachos into her mouth. As I was sitting down, I noticed that a lot of the other kids were looking and pointing out the windows.

When I turned to see what they were looking at, I saw the flashing blue lights from a couple of police cars. They were parked along the road where we got on and off the buses, and there were a bunch of policemen out there. I couldn't tell what they were doing, but all of them looked like they were worried about something.

"What's going on outside?" I sat and popped a nacho in my mouth. I was still really hungry.

"Dunno," Jaime answered with a mouthful of food. "But I heard that there's going to be some kind of special announcement after lunch."

"You mean like the one the principal already made?"

She shrugged.

Now that I knew they were out there, the flashing lights on the police cars seemed obvious. I watched them as I ate, plotting with Jaime how we could get back at Mrs. Green for taking my bear.

"Maybe we could put a whole bunch of that hand sanitizer she likes so much all over her chair, then when she sits down, she'll get a wet butt."

"Yeah!" Jaime liked that idea.

"But we'll have to make sure she doesn't know who did it, then she'd call my mom for sure, and maybe she'd keep Mr. Cuddles forever."

The bell rang and interrupted my revenge plans. I stood up and dumped my tray in the garbage can, leaving the tray in the growing stack by the door.

Mrs. Green was back at the door to our classroom with the hand sanitizer bottle when I got back to the room. I glared at the thing while she squirted some sanitizer on to my hands.

I had just made it to my desk when the loudspeaker crackled and the principal's voice came on again.

"An early dismissal has been announced for all schools in our district. Teachers are asked to escort their students to the auditorium and remain with them until a parent or guardian comes to pick them up. No students are to leave the building without a parent. There will be no buses today. All students must remain in the auditorium until a parent or guardian comes for them. No exceptions. Anyone showing signs of illness should report to the nurse. There will be no school on Monday. Classes are dismissed. Please report to the auditorium immediately."

There was a lot of talking as soon as the principal ended his announcement. One of the boys in the back row cheered. Chairs scraped back as the other kids jumped excitedly to their feet.

"That's enough! You are still in the school building, and you will remain calm and under control while you are here," Mrs. Green yelled with her unhappy face.

Everyone quieted down . . . a little. They began grabbing their bags from their cubbies and lining up at the door. I picked up my own bag and went to the end of the line. Mrs. Green was still trying to convince two boys to stop racing around the room and yelling about not having school on Monday.

I raised my hand.

"What, Luna?" My teacher's voice sounded like she was really annoyed.

"Um, could I have Mr. Cuddles back now?"

"Luna, can't you see I'm a little too busy to deal with your bear right now?"

"But you promised!" I said, raising my voice.

"Maybe you shouldn't have brought it to school where it doesn't belong then. You can have it back next week." She finally managed to herd the last of my classmates into line. "Now, let's go. Stay together and no talking in the halls."

It wasn't fair. She told me I could have Mr. Cuddles back at the end of the day. I wanted my bear. I never went anywhere without him.

When I was going to refuse to leave the room, the glare she sent my way made me change my mind. I would just tell my mommy when she came to get me. She would understand that I couldn't leave without my Mr. Cuddles.

CHAPTER THREE

Day Three

The auditorium was noisy when we walked into it. Teachers attempted to keep their students together, but the news that school was canceled for the rest of the day made most of the other kids wild.

I wasn't wild. I was too busy worrying about Mr. Cuddles. Was he scared all alone in that cold, dark desk drawer? As soon as Mommy got here, I was going to make sure she knew that we needed to rescue him right away.

"Over here. This way." Mrs. Green pointed at a row of empty seats.

I hated sitting in the auditorium. The seats were like the ones at the movies, and they didn't want to stay down when I sat on them. Mommy would laugh and tell me that I wasn't heavy enough yet, then she would put her hand on the seat so it stayed where it was supposed to. No one at the auditorium held the seat for me like Mommy did. It was uncomfortable.

The principal was up on the stage with a policeman. There was another policeman standing next to the doors. I had a funny feeling in my stomach. There was always a policeman outside when I got off the bus, but I had never seen one come into the school before.

While I watched, the policeman by the doors looked out into the hall, then pulled them closed. He nodded to the principal, and the microphone on the stage made that screeching noise it sometimes did when you first turn it on.

The teacher sitting with the class in front of ours slapped his hands over his ears and then massaged his forehead like Mommy had done this morning. When the noise stopped, he looked to the kids sitting to his right for a second, got up, and moved over a couple of seats.

I stopped watching the teacher when the principal started talking.

"Thank you for your cooperation. The announcements have been made asking parents to come for their students immediately. Our local police force are around to ensure that things run smoothly. We are asking parents to form two lines. When their ID is verified, I will call the student's name, and the student is then asked to go to their parent or guardian. Please do not loiter on school grounds when you are released. Teachers, when all of your students have been picked up, you may leave."

Taking the microphone with him, he jumped down from the stage and walked to the doors. The two ladies that I recognized from the office stood beside that policeman now. They each held some papers. When the principal shoved open the doors, I could see a bunch of people out in the hall.

The office ladies began talking to the people. They both started flipping through the papers in their hands. The one on the left side of the door, whom I liked because she always smiled at us when we saw her in the hallway, talked to the principal first.

"Conner Smith."

A boy near the back of the room jumped up and began happily climbing over everyone to get to an aisle. The lady standing next to the left side of the open door grabbed him as soon as he was close enough. She whirled around and dragged him through the door while he was still trying to wave to his friends. Conner's mommy didn't look very happy.

The principal kept calling names and it was getting really noisy in there. No matter how many times the teachers yelled to be quiet, everyone was just too excited to go home. Jaime's dad was one of the first parents to come. Jaime waved at me from over her dad's shoulder as he carried her through the crowd outside the door. Her older sister held on to the back of his shirt tightly as he pulled her along.

I wished Mommy would have been at the front of the line too. I just wanted to get Mr. Cuddles and go home. The parents outside of the door were starting to get loud too. Two more policemen came when one daddy tried to push his way into the room. He was yelling the name Sara a lot and waving his arms over his head. It was a little hard to tell, but it looked like his arm was bleeding.

The police pushed him back out of the auditorium while one of the office ladies stopped a girl in a blue shirt from bolting through the door. A police lady came and took the blue-shirt girl out into the hall.

Now, the parents outside were even noisier. They crowded close to the police. The office ladies were flipping through their papers as fast as they could, and the principal yelled names into the microphone so we could hear them. It was chaos, and it made the funny feeling in my tummy get worse.

It was starting to get quieter in the big auditorium. I didn't know if that was because a lot of kids had left or because the other kids were starting to get funny feeling in their tummies too. No one was laughing anymore.

Another girl from my class left. The boy who liked to pick his nose was the only one left sitting with Mrs. Green, except me. I saw a teacher leave, then another. Mrs. Green kept looking at us with her scrunched-up face look. I think she wanted us to go home as much as I wanted to see Mommy by the door.

When the teacher in the row in front of us suddenly stood up, I turned around to watch him. He swayed on his feet and almost fell down as he tried to hurry to an aisle.

"Mr. Baron, are you okay?" one of the kids who was in his class called when he tripped and fell.

He was on his hands and knees in the middle of the big aisle when he threw up.

"Ewww!" someone squealed.

Two policemen came then. They had on gloves like what a doctor wore. They helped the teacher up and then hurried him up toward the stage. He turned around to look back at his class when they took him to the door that was up there. He had vomit all over his face with funny-looking color.

Most of the kids were gone. It looked like there weren't very many parents still standing in line. I really wanted to hug Mr. Cuddles. Mommy was the only one who gave better hugs than my bear.

Where was Mommy? If the other kids' Mommies and Daddies knew to come get them, Mommy should come too. Mommy always came when I needed her.

"Could all of the students still in the auditorium please come sit in the last two rows?" the principal called.

I stayed a seat away from nose-picking boy because nose picking is gross. All of us fit into the last two rows of empty seats, so it was okay. There was enough room.

There were only five teachers left, and they stayed standing in a group in the aisle. Except for Mrs. Green. She stayed away from the other teachers and rubbed hand sanitizer on her hands. I wanted to tell her that Mommy said using too much hand sanitizer is bad for you.

The last mommy in the hall was crying. She hugged two boys when they went to her before they left. The only people still in the hall were policemen.

Where was Mommy?

I tried to look around them, to see her, but I didn't think she was out there. I hugged my pony backpack and wished it was Mr. Cuddles.

CHAPTER FOUR

Day One

Someone started shouting out in the hallway. The principal had been talking to the police by the door. When the shouting didn't stop, most of the police hurried from the room.

A policeman, the principal, the office ladies, and four of the teachers crowded around the door to watch what was happening in the hall.

Someone out there screamed. It was a funny-sounding scream that made me hug my backpack even tighter.

There was more shouting, then someone shot a gun. I knew it was a gun because I liked to sneak and watch movies at night that Mommy said I wasn't old enough to see. TV gunshots and real-life gunshots sounded a little different, but I knew that was a gunshot I heard.

More shouting and another scary scream. Some of the kids sitting near me were starting to cry, then there were more gunshots.

Suddenly, all the adults crowded in the door started to try to close the doors, but they were in each other's way and they couldn't get them shut. There was still a big gap when somebody crashed through and knocked most of them to the ground.

The person who crashed through the doors was the teacher who had thrown up in the aisle, but there was something wrong with him. He had something red smeared all over his face and his clothes. His shirt was unbuttoned and flew around him as he spun and darted. Mrs. Green had been the only one still standing partway down the aisle when he busted in. He saw her standing there and lunged at her, and the two of them crashed to the ground.

I had never seen a grown-up bite someone before, but that's what he did. He bit her right on one of her arms. Mrs. Green screamed.

So did some of the other kids. I was too scared to scream or cry. I hugged my pony backpack and wished it was Mommy while that teacher bit Mrs. Green again.

I was sorry I wished her head would explode. I was sorry I planned to squirt her hand sanitizer all over her chair. I wouldn't ever think mean thoughts about my teacher ever again if someone would just save her.

God must have thought that was a good deal because a policeman tackled the teacher who was biting Mrs. Green, then another one and another one.

The biting teacher was fighting with the police. He kept trying to bite and scratch them. He screamed another one of those awful screams, but more police came, and they held him down. He was still struggling when they dragged him out of the room.

Even nose-picking boy was crying now. Most of the other kids ran to their teachers. I was still in my seat. It felt like I couldn't move. I was having a hard time breathing.

"We have to get the kids out of here." A teacher with curly hair stopped the police lady.

Policemen were helping Mrs. Green sit in one of the seats. She was bleeding and crying.

The principal came over to where we were. "Alright, kids." He looked like he was going to throw up. "One bus is going to be here in just a few minutes. We are going to get on the bus and go somewhere a little safer while we wait for your parents." He started talking to the office lady next to him.

How would Mommy know where to come find me if I left the school? She always said to never leave school with anyone but her. Mommy was coming. She always came. Even if she didn't get the message like the other mommies and daddies, she would come to school to find me when I didn't come home on the bus like I was supposed to. I knew it. I just had to wait a little bit longer and she would be there.

I looked around. The four other teachers were trying to calm down the crying kids. Most of the policemen had left the auditorium. The principal and office ladies were busy looking at those papers again. People were wrapping some white cloth around Mrs. Green's arm.

No one was paying any attention to what I was doing.

I slid off my uncomfortable seat. When they ran away, the other kids mostly left their backpacks behind. If I crawled as far under the seats as I could go and put my backpack in front of me, maybe no one would notice that I was down there. I just had to hide until the principal left, then I could come back out. He said there would only be one bus. As long as I missed it, then I could stay here with the police and wait for Mommy to come.

The floor was cold. I curled up into as small of a ball as I could make anyhow and moved my backpack to a better spot. I held really, really still and hoped the principal would think I was just another backpack.

"How many students do you still have?" I heard his voice.

"Three."

"One."

"Three."

"Five."

The other teachers answered him.

"Does anyone know how many Mrs. Green still had?" I stopped breathing, afraid they would see me. "No? Hey, Mrs. Green is your teacher, right?"

"Yeah," gross nose-picking boy answered the principal.

"Is there anyone else from your class here?"

"No," he said. I started to breathe again.

There were some shuffling sounds, and the principal talked some more, but they didn't stay long. I heard some policemen tell them that it was time to leave.

Then it got really quiet in the auditorium. It was scary, but I had to stay hidden until I was sure that the bus was gone. I couldn't leave until Mommy came to get me.

I started counting. When the numbers got high enough that I couldn't remember what came next, I peeked out from behind my backpack. The auditorium was still really quiet. I was sure the bus was gone by now.

There was no one else in there when I stood up. I couldn't see any policemen out in the hall either. I went to the door and looked out.

There was red smeared on the white floor in a few places. Some pieces of trash littered the hall. A trash can was laying on its side with more trash coming out of it. The principal would be mad if he saw the mess. He was already going to be mad enough when he found out that I hid from him. I didn't want him to have even more reason to be mad.

I picked up the papers. One had something red on it and I got some on my hand when I picked it up. The red was a little sticky. I wiped it off on my pants.

It felt like it took a long time to clean up the mess. Whoever knocked over the trash can owed me. They should give me their dessert for a week. No, a month.

The police still hadn't come back. Whatever they were doing, it was taking a long time. Being alone in the school was scary and I really wanted to go home.

I was thirsty, so I got a drink from the water fountain in the hall.

I looked at the big pictures hanging way up high near the front doors. I recognized them. They were pictures of the teachers. I found Mrs. Green. When I found the picture of the teacher who bit Mrs. Green, I suddenly didn't feel like looking at the pictures anymore.

The picture of my teacher reminded me that Mr. Cuddles was still trapped in the desk drawer. I didn't know where everyone had gone, but at least, no one was there to stop me from taking him back.

It was a really long walk clear to the other end of the school. Some of the classroom's lights were off. I ran past the dark rooms so the scary things that might be inside wouldn't get me.

I closed the door to my classroom as quiet as I could when I finally got there.

I had never been happier to see Mr. Cuddles, and he was happy to see me, too, when I pulled him from the drawer.

"Mr. Cuddles, Mommy is coming. We just have to wait right here. She knows where Mrs. Green's class is." I hugged my bear to my chest and looked around the room.

I had never been the only one in the room before. That was scary too.

I sat at my desk, then Jaime's, then Mrs. Green's. That didn't make me feel better. I got out the crayons and colored a picture to give to Mommy. When my tummy growled, I remembered that I still had some fish crackers in my desk from snack time, and I ate them.

Mommy still wasn't there, but she was going to come soon. I was tired. We usually took a nap after lunch, but we went to the auditorium today instead. I went to my cubby and took out my blanket. I always took a nap in the corner of the room, so that's where I spread out my blanket. It was green like my favorite hair tie.

Mr. Cuddles snuggled up with me to take a nap while we waited for Mommy.

CHAPTER FIVE

Day Two

When we woke up, Mr. Cuddles and I were both hungry again. It felt like I slept for a really long time, but that couldn't be true because Mommy would have come looking for me.

Mrs. Green always kept the windows to her classroom covered because she said it would distract us to be able to look outside. The clock on the wall didn't mean anything to me. I needed another way to see how long I was asleep. Maybe if I only uncovered one window just a little, she wouldn't notice.

The colorful paper was taped over the windows, but I picked at a corner until I could peel it back enough to look out. It was dark out there. The sky was the color it was when Mommy would wake me up to go to school.

I had slept in the classroom all night!

Why hadn't the policemen come back from wherever they went to yet? And why didn't Mommy come find me?

My face was still pressed to the glass. There was something moving outside of the window. The sun wasn't making enough light yet and the outside was still shadowy.

Suddenly, a terrible face smacked into the window, eye to eye with me.

I shrieked and jumped away from the monster outside.

The man banged on the glass and showed his teeth to me. He had red all over his face and on his teeth and his eyes didn't look like people's eyes. The window rattled as he smacked his face into it again, looking in at me through the little hole I shouldn't have made in Mrs. Green's paper, then he opened his mouth wide and screamed.

He sounded like the teacher who bit Mrs. Green, and that was terrifying. I was afraid that he would want to bite me, too, if the glass wasn't in his way.

Grabbing Mr. Cuddles from where I had accidentally dropped him on the floor, I ran into our class bathroom. The door didn't have a lock, so I pushed my back up against it as hard as I could. I didn't want a monster man biting me like what had happened to my teacher.

The man outside banged on the window and screamed for a long time. After a while, I got tired of holding the door closed. Pushing on it so hard was making my legs tired.

I let go of the door and stepped away from it. Mr. Cuddles smelled like home, so I hugged him under my chin and waited for the monster man to come into the bathroom and get me.

When he didn't come, I sat on the potty and waited. I waited a long time, but I couldn't hear anyone making any noise out there anymore. Not the monster man. Not the policemen. Not Mommy.

My tummy growled really loud. I wanted breakfast. I would even eat cereal if there was some, but Mommy's pancakes sounded the best.

My tummy kept gurgling, and I guessed I was going to have to find my own breakfast. There was a fast-thumping sound in my ears when I let the bathroom door go open. My heart was as afraid as I was. The classroom was just as empty as it was before. Luckily, the monster man wasn't banging on the window anymore.

I looked at the spot of window that I had uncovered. I should cover it back up but going back over there was too scary. Mrs. Green was just going to have to go ahead and get mad at me when she came back, because I wasn't fixing her window. The monster man was scarier than she was.

The fish crackers were all gone, and Mommy hadn't put any more snacks in my backpack. I checked in my desk and found a half of a granola bar I had forgotten I put in there. I was hungry enough to eat cereal, so I ate the granola bar even though there was a piece of fuzzy stuck to it. I was still hungry.

Some of my friends ate breakfast in the cafeteria before school started. I never did, but I knew sometimes Jaime ate there if her Mommy was in a hurry to go to work. She said their cereal was gross and they never had good stuff like pancakes, and I was always secretly happy that I never had to eat breakfast at school.

The school was so quiet that I was pretty sure the lunch ladies weren't there either, but I knew how to pour cereal and milk into a bowl. I could get my own breakfast if I went to the cafeteria.

"Mr. Cuddles, we're gonna go to the cafeteria now. Okay?"

My bear didn't say no, so I went to the classroom door. My heart was making that thumping sound again when I pushed the door open far enough to peek out. The hall was empty.

I always talked to Mr. Cuddles, but something made me not want to make any noise as I tried to sneak past the classrooms with open doors. The rooms with the lights off were the worst. I stopped before each one as I hurried past as fast as I could without my shoes making noise on the floor. The monster man's scary eyes made me go faster down the hall. *What if he was waiting in one of the dark rooms to get me?*

It was light outside now. When I got to the doors out to where the bus always waited for us, I slowed down and looked outside. There were two grown-ups out there. They stood over by the flagpole, looking up at the flag as it waved in the wind. I tripped over my own foot; I was so excited to see them. Maybe one of them would take me home to see Mommy.

They stood really still, and I stopped just before my hands pushed on the bar to open the door. Their backs were to me, but those grown-ups made me scared of them. I didn't know why, but I suddenly didn't want them to know I was there. I took my hands off the door and started backing up, keeping watch on them. They just stood there, staring at that flag like it was doing something a whole lot more interesting than just flapping in the wind.

When a siren started making noise from somewhere out there, I jumped and made a squeak noise. I clapped a hand over my mouth to stop more noise from coming out and looked at the grown-ups, afraid that they heard me.

They must not have though, because both of them took off so fast, running past the school doors and out of sight. I thought they were running towards the sound of the siren.

There was something not right about how they ran. I was right to be scared of them, they reminded me of the monster man even though I never saw their faces.

The daylight made me feel a little better. The dark was scary, but every story that Mommy ever read me always said that there were no monsters in the light, but I just saw two of them, and there was light outside. The stories were wrong. Monsters could come out in the daytime too.

CHAPTER SIX

Day Two

  I never went into the kitchen at school before. The lunch ladies always stood back there while putting food on the shiny countertop, wearing silly nets over their hair that made me giggle the first time I saw them. Kids weren't supposed to go back there. I looked all around me to be sure that no one was going to jump out and yell at me before I went around the end of the counter.

  The lights were left on, and everything was made out of the same shiny metal. The glare hurt my eyes. "Don't look, Mr. Cuddles." I turned him around so the bright lights wouldn't hurt his eyes too.

  It didn't look like our kitchen at home. It took me a second to figure out where the refrigerator was. When I opened it up, I found a bunch of those little cartons of milk that we always got with our lunch instead of a gallon of milk. I took one and closed the door. A little more looking around the kitchen and I found a shelf that was stacked high with cereal in little plastic cups.

I hadn't found a spoon yet, but being in the shiny kitchen was making me have that funny feeling in my tummy again. I took my milk and my cereal and went back out into the cafeteria.

My shoes echoed on the hard floor when I walked to the table that I usually sat at to eat lunch with Jaime. It was so quiet in the school without all the other kids. It would have made me really happy if there was someone else there too. Even Mrs. Green.

Mr. Cuddles watched me eat my cereal. I looked out the window while I ate. Every once in a while, I saw someone out the window, but I was too afraid of finding out that whoever was out there was a monster too, so I stayed in my seat and didn't try to get their attention. At least, by the time I finished my cereal and milk, my tummy was finally full. Grabbing Mr. Cuddles, I took my trash and dropped it into the full garbage can.

The lunch ladies hadn't emptied it from lunch yesterday. The trash was starting to smell bad. I wrinkled my nose and walked away from the cans. Looking around the brightly lit cafeteria, I couldn't find any reason to stay in that room, so I went back out into the hall. When Mommy came, I was sure she would look for me in my classroom first, so that was where I should stay anyhow.

I was walking past the front doors again when a loud bang on the glass made me jump. Turning around fast, I found someone on the other side of the door, watching me with those scary monster man eyes. She wasn't much bigger than I was, but she screeched and banged against the doors, making lots of noise. I hugged Mr. Cuddles to my chest and watched the monster girl, too afraid to move.

She made so much noise that before long, another monster came and started banging on the door too. My eyes got really big when I saw that it was Jaime's mommy. She had a big scratch down her face that bled all over her shirt, and she spit all over the window as she shrieked at me through the glass, but that was Jaime's mommy, even if I had never seen her be anything but quiet and nice.

Seeing her act like the other monsters made me want to cry. I didn't know what was wrong with her, but Jaime's mommy would have never acted like this. I just wanted things to go back to the way they were supposed to be.

I started backing away from the doors. I didn't want to see them anymore. Hiccupping a little, I held on to my bear and kept watching them as I started to get further down the hall. The two monsters outside tried to follow me, moving along the row of glass doors to stay as close to me as they could get. I was almost far enough down the hall that I couldn't see them anymore when Jaime's mommy monster bumped the little girl monster, sending her tumbling to the side.

The girl monster crashed into the wall and directly onto the blue button there that the boy who was in a wheelchair used to open the doors.

The doors started to slowly swing open.

The mommy monster came in the doors first. Her eyes locked on me down the hall, and she started running towards me as fast as she could go.

I was so scared as I turned around and started running towards my classroom. I went as fast as I could go. I held on to Mr. Cuddles with one hand while I ran, but when I looked behind me, the mommy monster was closer. She was faster than I was, and I knew that she was going to catch me before I made it all the way back to Mrs. Green's room.

I didn't want to get bitten by a monster person. I had to find a place to hide from them until they went away. There was a classroom with its lights still on and its door open ahead of me. I dove inside it and whirled around to pull the heavy door closed. The mommy monster was still running as fast as she could go, and her red monster eyes were so close to me when I finally got the door to start swinging closed.

The door was still a little bit open when she crashed into it, slamming it the rest of the way closed. I dropped Mr. Cuddles and used both hands to hold onto the doorknob, afraid that the monsters would try to open the door. I had seen Mrs. Green use a key to lock and unlock our classroom door before, but I didn't have a key, and I didn't have a way to lock the door. The hiccupping was worse as I held on as tight as I could, waiting to feel the door try to go open.

The door stayed shut. On the other side, the mommy monster screamed and banged against the door. A few seconds later, the girl monster started banging on the door, too, but they must have forgotten how to use a doorknob because the door didn't move.

I really was crying, then sniffing because crying always made my nose want to run. I was hanging on to the door with both hands. The monsters kept banging and screaming out in the hall, and all I wanted was for Mommy to come get me and take me home.

CHAPTER SEVEN

Day Three

It was morning again.

The monsters outside the room had been quiet for a long time. I held on to the doorknob for what felt like forever, but they never figured out how to open the heavy wooden door. I had to give up holding the door eventually. I scooped up Mr. Cuddles from where he had been watching me from the floor and hugged him as I backed away from the door.

They were still out there, but it sounded like they were wandering around the hall instead of trying to crash through the door. I stayed as quiet as a mouse as I went to sit behind the teacher's desk.

This classroom was for some of the big kids, and it was a lot less interesting than my classroom. There weren't any colorful pictures on the walls or anything like that, and the big kids didn't eat a snack or take a nap either. I had figured that out when I snuck around the room looking for lunch and later when I really wanted a blanket to take a nap.

I found some candy in the teacher's desk drawer, but the door closed with a loud click, making me wish that I never looked in there because the noise made the monsters start banging on the door again.

They kept it up out there for hours, even after it got dark outside again. I had eventually eaten the teacher's candy before crawling under the desk with Mr. Cuddles to sleep.

When I woke up again, the sun was up. I was too cold from laying on the bare floor all night.

It was silent out in the hallway.

I figured out another thing that made the big kid's room different from mine. They didn't have their own bathroom. I had been too afraid to leave my hiding spot behind the desk after the monsters started trying to get in the second time. I was too afraid that if I made more noise, they would hear me, but now, I really, really needed to use the potty.

I climbed out from under the desk and looked around the room a little desperately. The only door was the one to the hall, and there was no way I was going back out there.

Mommy wouldn't have been proud of what I did next . . . because I went to the farthest corner of the room and peed right on the floor.

That's how I noticed that one of my laces was untied. The laces got all wet from the puddle on the floor. When I walked, they flopped around and slapped wetly against my leg.

I started to cry again because I was lonely, hungry, and missed Mommy, and I had pee on me. I sat on the floor and cried and cried into my bear until the tears ran out and I couldn't cry anymore.

All that crying I did made Mr. Cuddles as wet as my shoelaces. I didn't feel any better, and now, my cuddly bear was all soggy. I pushed up off the floor and went back to the teacher's desk. I sat Mr. Cuddles up on the corner so he could dry off and pulled the teacher's chair out to sit in.

It was one of those fun chairs that can spin around.

I spun one way in the chair and then the other until I was so dizzy, I almost fell right out of the seat.

I drew pictures on some papers on top of the desk. Pictures of dogs and ponies and a big picture of Mommy and me at the park.

I tried to ignore how thirsty and hungry I was and the idea that I was going to have to pee on the floor again if someone didn't come to get me out of this room soon.

By the time I was tired of spinning and drawing and wondering where everyone had gone, Mr. Cuddles was dry enough to hold again. Happily scooping him up, I silently told him that everything was going to be okay.

I figure he could probably tell what I was saying, even if I couldn't say it out loud. Kid's bears are special like that.

What I didn't tell him was that I was starting to get worried about Mommy. She should have come looking for me a long time ago. She never would have forgotten that I needed to come home from school.

Mommy had been sick when I got on the school bus. What if she was too sick to get out of bed? What if Mommy was all alone at home, sick, with no one to take care of her?

I was starting to think that Mr. Cuddles and I were going to have to find our own way home.

I had no idea how we were going to do that though. I couldn't even get out of this room. The monsters out in the hall had been quiet all day, but I was sure they were still out there. Maybe they were hiding in one of the dark classrooms, waiting for me to come out.

    I wandered over to the windows and looked out. I didn't think the classroom windows opened, but maybe if I could figure out how, that would be a way out of the school.

    Some of my hair was in my face. My green hair tie was gone. I didn't know when I lost it. Shoving the red stuff out of my face, I looked out the window.

    A few birds flew across the blue sky. I could see some smoke going up into the air, coming from some houses that my bus always drove by in the morning. There was someone laying in the field where we played kickball at recess, not moving.

    I didn't see any monsters out there. If I was going to try to get out the window, maybe I should do it now before more of them showed up.

    The school windows didn't look like our windows at home. There was no latch that you had to turn before you could open them. I didn't see any kind of latch at all.

    I looked all over the windows but couldn't find a way to open them. I pushed at them, tried prying them up, but they stayed stubbornly closed.

    These windows didn't open. Slumping my shoulders, I went back to sit in the spinning chair. If I wasn't going to be able to get out the window, then I was just going to have to go out in the hall.

    But not before I tied my shoelaces. Mommy always said I would trip if my shoes were untied. I didn't want to trip if I had to run from the monsters again.

Pulling my foot up onto the chair in front of me, I looked at the laces. They were dirty from me walking on them and from getting peed on. I hesitantly poked one to see if it was still wet.

Nope. Dry. That didn't mean I wanted to touch them though. I tried using just the tips of my fingers to tie them, but it wasn't working. It didn't help that I didn't really know how to tie my own shoes.

Mommy had been trying to teach me. Closing my eyes, I tried to remember how her hands looked when she tied the laces.

My attempt to do what she did didn't work. The loops fell apart as soon as I let go of them.

I was trying to get the loops to stay in place for what must have been the hundredth time when a scary howl echoed down the hall. I jumped in the chair and held really still, waiting to see what would happen next.

A squeaky shriek sounded. That must be what the monster girl sounded like.

The monsters were talking to each other.

I went back to working on the laces. I had to get this shoe tied so I could go home.

CHAPTER EIGHT

Day Four

It was morning again.

Again.

My lips felt like they did that time I got a bad sunburn and Mommy put some cool, green lotion on me. I tried licking them, but it didn't help. I was so thirsty.

I was going to have to leave the room and find a drink. There was a water fountain in the hall. I just had to make it that far without the monsters hearing me.

I had to leave anyhow. I needed to get home to take care of Mommy. If I could make it to get a drink from the water fountain, maybe I could make it all the way out the front door.

I was sure I could do it.

If I could tie my own shoelaces, I could leave the school.

It took me a bazillion tries, but my shoe was finally tied. The bow wasn't pretty and even like when Mommy did it, but it had stayed tied even when I swung my foot around and shook it to try to make the bow come loose.

I couldn't wait to get home and show Mommy that she didn't have to tie my shoes anymore. She was going to be so proud. Maybe even proud enough to not mind too much that I had gone to the bathroom on the floor like I was a bad puppy or something.

Maybe I just wouldn't admit to anyone that it was me who messed the floor. No one had seen me do it. If I didn't tell anyone, this teacher never needed to know who stole her candy and peed on the floor.

Feeling a little better because no one would ever know that I was the one who made the mess, I crept to the door and listened. The monsters were still out there. They woke me up in the night with their screeching, but the sounds sounded like they were coming from further away. They weren't staying right outside the classroom door anymore.

Tucking Mr. Cuddles under one arm securely, I slowly turned the doorknob. My heart was scared again, pounding away in my chest. I was sure that as soon as the door opened just a little bit, one of the monsters would be there, ready to try to bite me.

The door opened with a quiet sound. I pushed it a few inches, then a few more when nothing bad happened. It swung open almost all the way.

The hallway was still brightly lit, but it didn't look the same. Some of the art projects that had been stuck to the walls were now on the floor. They were ripped and crumpled. A brownish smear stained the wall right in front of me. The hallway was completely silent, but it felt like someone was watching from the shadows, waiting for me to step into a trap.

I got stuck in the doorway. My feet didn't want to move. I held on to my bear and tried to convince him that everything was going to be okay. We just had to get a drink and then get out through the front doors.

The first step out into the hallway was scary. The second even more so. I just wanted to run back into the classroom and close the door, but I made my feet keep going. The open doors and darkened rooms were so much scarier this time than before. Now I knew that there really were monsters hiding around there somewhere, I just didn't know where.

The water fountain was getting closer, shiny like the school kitchen had been shiny and just waiting there for me to come get a drink. I hurried the last couple of steps.

When I got to the fountain, I stopped to look around, but I was still the only one in the hall. Putting Mr. Cuddles down on the little ledge at the back of the fountain, I pressed the big button on the front.

The machine came on with a quiet hum, and a stream of water came out. It came out a little too fast, and some of the water flew out of the fountain and made a wet spot on the floor. I let go of the button and then pushed it again, less hard this time.

I had never been so happy to see plain old water before in my life. I started drinking as much of it as I could.

I was so busy drinking the water, I forgot to watch out for the monsters for a second. When I heard the footsteps, they were already close. I looked up just in time to see the little monster girl running down the hall towards me.

I turned around and ran. She was right behind me.

She was so close to me that she slipped in the water on the floor and crashed into the side of the water fountain with a big bang.

The noise was really loud. I was running back down the hall, trying to get back to my safe classroom, when Jaime's mommy monster came out into the light ahead of me.

She showed me her yucky teeth and then charged towards me.

The little girl monster was back on her feet behind me. I could hear her running too. I was never going to make it back to my class; one of them would catch me before I got there.

The art room door was open to my right. I ran inside and slammed the door, then I stared at the door with wide eyes because I forgot that the art room door was glass, not heavy and solid like the regular classroom doors. If the monsters banged on this door like they did the last one, they were going to get in.

The room was big and was covered from one end to the other in half-finished art projects. It hung from strings on the ceiling. It covered most of the tables. The room was full of colorful papers that blew in the wind I made when I ran past. I had to find a better hiding place.

There was a big closet at the back of the room. I had been in there one time when the art teacher asked me to get more paint for the class. That was where I was running to. I was almost there when something slammed into the glass art door.

The door rattled and made a cracking sound. I didn't look back. One of the monsters screamed, and a second bang on the door made the cracking sound worse.

The art closet door was right there. I grabbed it and pulled it open and ran inside even though it was dark. Another bang and I heard glass hitting the tile floor. I yanked the closet door closed, closing myself in darkness.

There was a loud crash out in the room that sounded like one of the monsters tripped over a desk. I backed away from the door until I bumped into a shelf, then I stood really still.

The closet door banged when the monsters ran into it.

This door was heavy like the other classroom doors, so they banged and scratched and screamed, but they couldn't get through it. Listening to the sounds they made while being in the dark was even more scary than listening to their sounds in the light. I knew where the light switch was from the time I had been in there before, and I turned it on so I would feel a little better.

The closet was big and colorful with all the art stuff, but it was still just a closet. I scooted all the way to the back corner and sat on the floor. I sat there for a while, watching the door for any sign that the monsters were going to get in.

It was cold and uncomfortable, and I really wished I had something soft to hold, because I left Mr. Cuddles on the water fountain when I ran from the monsters.

CHAPTER NINE

Day Six

The closet was hot and stuffy. It was starting to smell really bad. I needed to get out of there, to go home, but I could still hear one of the monsters knocking things over out in the art room.

I needed to get home to Mommy. I didn't know how long I had been hiding in this closet, but it felt like a really long time. I was so thirsty again, and my tummy had given up complaining that it wanted food; it wasn't even growling anymore.

When I stood up from where I had been staring at the colorful little scraps of paper that littered the floor, casualties of me being bored, my head felt funny. I almost tipped over sideways and had to use a shelf to hold myself up for a minute.

I was almost desperate enough to open the door even knowing what was still on the other side. Almost.

I looked around the closet again, but nothing had changed. The only way out was through the door.

A slightly muffled scream came from out in the art room, and the monster crashed into something again, then I heard the best sound in the world. I heard someone talking.

"It's in here. Watch it!"

There were some more noises like the monster tripped over some chairs, then one loud bang. A gun. It got really quiet out in the art room after that.

I stood right next to the closet door, but I didn't open it. There were strangers out there, and as happy as I was that there were finally other people in the school, Mommy had always warned me to be careful around strangers. What if they weren't nice people? So I stood next to the door, but I didn't open it.

A scuffling sound, then I heard, "There's not going to be anything we want in here, Maggie. Let's get out of here. Let's see if we can find the nurse's office without running into any more dead people."

"Yeah, you're probably right. I doubt they kept anything to clean up a wound in an art class. Just give me one second."

There was a man and a woman out there. I could hear them moving around if I listened hard enough.

"Charlie's gonna think we got eaten. Let's go, Maggie, before she gives up and leaves without us."

"She won't leave us, not without being sure that we're gone. Besides, Jess needs something to clean up that cut, or it's going to get infected." There was a long pause. "Alright. Let me see what's behind this door, and we'll move on."

The door opened so fast that I didn't even have time to hide. Not that there was any place to hide in the closet anyhow.

The light outside the closet was so much brighter, even though I had the light switch turned on this whole time. I blinked and tried to see the people who were staring back at me with surprised expressions on their faces.

"What the h*ll!" the man said. He had brown hair and brown eyes, and he looked a little familiar, like I must have seen him somewhere before. I decided right away that I liked him, even if he did say a bad word.

I stayed where I was in the closet, not sure if I should try to run. The lady, who had brown hair, too, and was kinda tall, crouched down so we were the same height. "I guess we know why it was making such a mess of this room." She looked at the man while she said it, then looked back at me. "Hey, hun. It's okay. You can come out now."

I didn't move.

The lady looked back at her friend. "I'm Maggie. This is my friend Colton. What's your name?" she said.

When I didn't answer her, she asked, "Is there anyone else here?"

I shook my head.

"Okay, sweetie. You'd better come with us. It's not safe for you to stay here alone."

The lady, Maggie, stayed crouched down and reached towards me with a hand. I looked from her to Colton and back again.

I really didn't want to be alone anymore.

"Have to stay here and wait for Mommy." My voice didn't even sound like me. I tried licking my dry lips, but it didn't work.

The two grown-ups looked at each other again before Maggie stood up with her hand still extended. "Sweetie, I can't stay here with you. I have a friend, she's hurt, and I need to find her the medicine she needs. She's waiting outside with our other friend. Their names are Jess and Charlie. Colton and I have to go back to help keep them safe. It's better to be with other people now. We can keep you safe too."

"Your Mommy will want you to be safe until she can get back to you," Colton told me.

He was right. Mommy always said to be safe, no matter what I was doing. She always reminded me to make good choices.

I thought that going with these people may be making a good choice. It was so hard to tell.

Making up my mind, I reached out and grabbed ahold of Maggie's hand.

She smiled at me. "Okay. Let's get out of here and see if we can find the nurse's office to this place."

It felt weird, stepping out of the closet, like something big happened, but I didn't know what.

Maggie and Colton tried to block the mommy monster, so I couldn't see her laying on the floor. I knew it was her because Jaime had the same hair as her mommy. I saw some of that hair, then I thought of something.

"Where's the other one?" I looked up at Maggie.

She looked back at me. "There's another one of them here?"

I nodded. "The little girl monster. She chased me too."

"Oh, man." Colton sounded upset. "I don't know if I can shoot a dead kid. It's a kid."

"Yeah." Maggie started walking again and tugged me along behind her. "Let's get out of here. We'll find what we need somewhere else."

There were pieces of broken glass on the floor and lots of broken art projects. The tables and chairs weren't sitting in straight lines anymore. My school didn't look like my school. Suddenly, I was really glad that I was getting away from it, even if I wasn't going with Mommy.

She would find me, I was sure of it. I just had to stay safe until she came.

"The door's back this way, I think."

Colton was walking a little ahead of us. He was going the right way, so I stayed quiet. The hallway was a little less scary now that I wasn't alone.

I had never been so happy to see Mr. Cuddles when the water fountain appeared ahead of us. I bounced on my feet a little when he was safely back under my arm. We were almost back to the front doors when I heard the sound that I least wanted to hear.

The little girl monster's shrill scream came from behind us.

"Crap!" Colton muttered as he swung around to look back.

"Crap!" he said again. "Go! She's pretty far back there. We might be able to beat her to the doors."

Maggie picked me right up and started running. I could see the girl monster over her shoulder. She was running down the hall, but my new friend Maggie was tall, and she could run fast. The girl monster was just passing the water fountain when Maggie rushed us through the front doors.

Behind her, Colton pushed the door shut as fast as he could, and the girl monster bounced off the glass when she hit it.

Maggie put me down on the sidewalk, and we all stood there for a second, watching the girl monster as she bit and scratched at the inside of the door.

"Jesus," Colton said.

"Yeah," Maggie agreed.

I didn't really know what they meant, but I was glad to be outside of my school.

"Well, what do ya say we find you something to eat and drink, kiddo? You have to be hungry." Maggie looked down at me and held out her hand again.

I nodded. Tucking Mr. Cuddles back under my arm, he had almost fallen out when we were running, so I took her hand. I thought that I was pretty lucky to have made new friends like Maggie and Colton. I thought that Mommy would have been proud of me. There was just one thing that I needed to tell them.

"My name is Luna."

Do you like dystopian stories?
Here are samples of other stories
you might enjoy!

THE FIRST 30 DAYS

LORA POWELL

ONE
DAY 1

The trail of green slime worked its way down her face, moving steadily closer to her mouth. Like when you passed an accident on the highway and you knew you didn't really want to see any dead bodies, but you still found yourself looking anyhow, I couldn't pull my gaze from the horror unfolding in front of me.

The oblivious mother was at the other end of the cart, throwing groceries onto the belt as fast as her arms could move. Strapped into the seat, the blonde-haired toddler clutched a stuffed pink elephant that was missing an eye and watched me with equal fascination as I showed her. Big blue eyes lit up with curiosity when I shifted my overloaded shopping basket to my other hand.

The thick snot inched closer to her upper lip. I eyed it, not sure if I should say something to the mom. Moms didn't like unsolicited advice, right? Especially from twenty-year-olds who had never changed a diaper in their life.

My inner conflict was solved when the girl's tongue swept out and the green streak disappeared.

Holding back the urge to gag, I looked anywhere but at the kid.

The store was packed.

Why did I always manage to come do my shopping at the busiest times?

You would think I would learn not to shop on a Friday night. The lines were long, resulting in the painful wait behind the snot nosed kid I was currently experiencing.

A large red sign hanging over the pharmacy advertised flu shots. Glancing back at the girl, I wondered if I should fork over the cash and get one. I never had before, but I really couldn't afford to miss any work, and the news stations were calling this year's flu an epidemic.

The line wrapping around the pharmacy counter was what finally convinced me to skip the vaccine for now. I'd already suffered inside this grocery store long enough for one day and that line looked like there had to be dozens of people in it.

Finally, enough room appeared on the belt for me to put my groceries up. Flexing my shoulder, I tried to rid myself of the soreness that my heavy basket had caused. Thankfully, the mother was now blocking my view of her sick daughter.

After a few more minutes spent reading about the new president's policies—policies that had the country melting down—on the tabloids strategically placed at eye level, it was my turn.

"Thank you for shopping with us today. Did you find everything okay?" the bored cashier mumbled as she began scanning my things. She didn't even look up.

"Sure, I…" I trailed off. The woman didn't actually care and wasn't really listening. Not that I blamed her.

How many times a day was she forced to repeat that idiotic greeting?

I swiped my card and picked up my bags, stepping into the steady flow of shoppers leaving the store. Out in the packed parking lot, I found my ten-year-old Honda and jumped inside. All I really wanted to do was get home, put my food away, and curl up on the couch in my comfy pajamas. Netflix was calling me.

The house I shared with my roommate was only a few minutes away from the store and in no time, I was parking my car. The short driveway barely had enough room for both of our cars so I parked carefully because I didn't want to bump her car again.

Once done, I lugged the bags up the sidewalk and through the unlocked front door.

"Evie!" I put one armload down long enough to twist the lock behind me. "You left the door unlocked again!"

My roommate was pretty good, as far as roommates went but she frequently forgot to lock the door behind herself, which was a pet peeve of mine.

"Sorry!" Evie's head of red curls appeared at the top of the steps. "I was thinking about what to wear tonight. I must have forgotten." She ducked back out of sight.

Sighing, I carried my bags to the kitchen and dumped them on the small table. Evie was never going to change, and I'd figured that out at some point during the nearly two years we had lived under the same roof. Restocking my shelf in the fridge with my purchases, I tossed the balled up plastic bags in the trash and headed upstairs. An oversized pair of ugly flannel pjs, a bag of chips, and binge watching my favorite pair of brothers were my only plans for the night.

Evie darted out of our shared bathroom, still putting an earring in her ear and I jumped back to avoid a collision.

"Sorry!" She smiled brightly at me. "What do you think?"

Wearing a slinky black dress that barely covered her backside and sky-high heels that I would be guaranteed to break an ankle in, Evie was dressed for a good time.

"Going out with Austin?" For once, she was dating a guy that I actually liked. Evie's usual type was jerk.

"Yeah. He's taking me out for our second month anniversary." She flashed her dark lined eyes at me and grinned.

"You look great, Evie. Have fun." As I was talking, I noticed a Band-Aid in her upper arm. "What's that?"

Noticing the direction I was looking at, Evie gasped. "Oh! Thank goodness you noticed. I forgot." Reaching up, she pulled the Band-Aid off. "I went and got a flu shot today over my lunch break."

"I almost got one today too, but the line was too long."

"Yeah. I was almost late clocking back in. It took so long. At least, now I shouldn't get sick."

Three loud knocks on the door downstairs cut our conversation short. Waving goodbye, she rapidly bounced down the steps and I heard the door open. My room was the last door in the hall, and I walked there as I heard her happily greeting her boyfriend.

The next couple of hours were spent drooling over Dean and stuffing my face with junk food. I was sprawled out on our lumpy couch, almost asleep, when I heard the sound of the front door opening. Pulled from my food coma, I sat up far enough to see who was coming in over the back of the couch. Only three people had a key: Evie, me, and our landlord. But it never failed to make me nervous when someone came in the door. You could never be too careful.

Austin appeared, an arm around Evie's waist as if he was supporting her as they came into the room.

"Here you go." He helped her into the recliner.

Awake now, I sat up all the way. "What's wrong guys?"

"Evie's not feeling so great."

"I'm fine. I'm just feeling a little dizzy." She swayed a bit as she attempted to smile at me.

Evie didn't actually look fine. Her normally pale skin looked even more washed out, except for her flushed cheeks.

"You don't look fine, Evie. Maybe we should take your temperature."

She waved my suggestion away. "No. Don't worry. I just need to sleep this off. Must be that danged flu shot. That'll be the last time I get one of those." She looked up to where her boyfriend was still hovering next to her chair. "Help me upstairs?"

The two of them slowly made their way up to Evie's room. I was awake now, but no longer in a Netflix kind of mood. It wasn't like my friend to get sick.

I picked up the mess I'd made in the living room and ran into Austin as he came back down the stairs. He left after soliciting a promise from me to keep an eye on Evie for the night. Not that he needed to ask; I planned to check in on her anyhow. But it was nice to finally see Evie with someone who was concerned about her.

Up in my room, I put away the basket of laundry that had been sitting by my closet for three days. Then deciding to check on Evie before climbing into bed, I crept to her door and opened it as silently as I could. I didn't want to wake her up if she was asleep.

Covered with a pile of warm blankets, Evie shifted restlessly but appeared to be sleeping. After sneaking a glass of water and some Ibuprofen onto her night stand, I quietly closed her door and went back to my own room.

TWO
DAY 2

An ambulance siren sounding much closer than usual was what finally pulled me awake. Wiping the sleep from my eyes, I rolled out of bed and went to my window. I had to blink a few times to straighten out my blurred vision, but finally, the ambulance disappearing down the end of our street came into focus.

It was an odd sight.

While I didn't exactly live in a gated community, the neighborhood was quiet. I think the only other time I could remember emergency services on this street was the time Mr. Johnson had a heart attack after shoveling his sidewalk. I really hoped whoever was taking the ride to the hospital this time fared better than Mr. Johnson had.

I stretched my arms over my head, fully awake.

Sleep deprived was never a good look on me, and I had gotten up a couple of times in the night to check on Evie. She had slept through the night though somewhat restlessly. On my last check, I had noticed the fever meds and water I'd left by her bed were gone. I was happy to see that. I didn't risk actually touching her to know for sure, but the flushed color of her cheeks suggested that Evie was running a fever.

Remembering her state, I searched for the thermometer. I knew that we kept it around somewhere, and rummaging in the bathroom cabinet finally produced the elusive object. Walking silently, I went to Evie's bedroom and placed the thermometer along with more water and Ibuprofen next to her. Then I shut myself in our bathroom down the hall for my morning shower.

When I turned off the hair dryer, a mild thump from Evie's room told me that she was awake. Throwing on a pair of jeans and a sweatshirt, I opened the door, eager to talk to her and see how she was feeling. The news had been saying that this year's flu was a particularly nasty strain. I was hoping that wasn't what was wrong with my roommate.

Mentally kicking myself for not getting that flu shot the night before, I lightly knocked on her closed door. A groan answered me.

I guess Evie is still sick.

Frowning, I pushed her door open.

"Evie?"

Inside her room was dark. She must have pulled the curtains while I was in the shower.

I could make out her huddled form on the bed and stepped closer to her bedside. "How are you feeling?"

The form on the bed suddenly rolled over.

Flinging one arm over her eyes and the other waving in the air, she groaned again. "Check for yourself."

Her voice came out raspy and strained and with her waving hand, she pointed toward her nightstand.

Realizing that she was pointing at the thermometer, I picked it up. My eyes practically bugged out of my skull.

105°F.

Was that even possible?

"Evie, I don't think this thermometer is working."

"Oh, it's working. You should feel how I feel."

Reaching down, I touched the back of my hand to Evie's arm. Jerking back in surprise, I just stared at my friend for a few seconds. She was burning up. I'd never felt heat like that coming from a person's skin before.

"Hon, we need to take you to a doctor."

She weakly waved me off. "No doctor. I can't afford my deductible. I'll be okay. I just need to sleep."

"Evie, a fever this high is dangerous."

"Please let me sleep, Bri." She groaned. "Can you text Austin for me?"

I watched her for a minute, torn about what to do. Evie was really sick, but she was a grown woman too. She had the right to make her own decisions.

Reaching down, I pulled the comforter back over her huddled body. "Okay. I'll text him."

* * *

By midmorning, I was really worried about Evie. She hadn't moved from the position I left her in. I texted Austin, and within 20 minutes, he was knocking at our front door.

"Hey, she's asleep upstairs." I closed the door behind him.

Austin's worried brown eyes met mine before he turned to look up the steps. "Has she been awake at all?"

"Not since earlier this morning. Her fever was really high, but she didn't want to go to the hospital."

I crossed my arms in front of myself. I had been second guessing my decision to follow Evie's wishes all morning.

"Yeah. She's stubborn when she wants to be. I'm going to go check on her."

I watched as he bounded up the stairs. Then I went back into the living room and decided to turn on the news. The news anchor was going over the same story that they had been running for a couple of days, urging everyone to get their flu shot. When she started reciting statistics on the number of children who had died already this year, I muted the TV. I'd already heard it yesterday and didn't really want to hear about dead kids again.

Austin's footsteps coming down the stairs alerted me to his return. "She's asleep." He sat in the chair. "She looks really bad, Bri."

"Yeah. I know. I don't know what to do. She said no doctor, but I've never seen anyone that sick."

Leaning forward, he rested his elbows on his knees. "I think she needs to go to the hospital. She's going to be mad, but I really think it's what needs to happen."

Austin was right, and I knew it. I'd been thinking the same thing myself. Luckily, Evie and I went to the same doctor. Nodding, I pulled my phone from my pocket and dialed. She was just going to have to get over being mad because I was making her an appointment.

I sat, impatiently tapping a foot as I listened to the phone ring and ring. Suddenly, the line went dead. Frowning,

I redialed. The phone rang for an uncommonly long time again before a stressed sounding woman finally answered.

"Family Medical Group, this is Lisa. How can I help you?"

"Hi, Lisa. I need to make an appointment for Evie Edwards. She's a patient of Dr. Gordon and she needs to be seen today."

"Ma'am, I'm sorry. Our schedule is full for today." Lisa, the receptionist, didn't even hesitate to deliver the news.

"I know it's short notice, but she really needs to be seen."

Sudden loud talking in the background made it difficult to hear Lisa as she rushed on to say, "I'm sorry. We are already overbooked. This flu is brutal. If Ms. Edwards is really ill, my best suggestion for you is to take her to the ER."

Getting desperate, I tried again. "But I don't think you—" I was cut off by a shrill scream coming through the phone. Then the line went dead again.

Who on earth was screaming in the doctor's office?

"She hung up on me," I told Austin incredulously.

The two of us just sat there, staring at each other. What were we supposed to do now? If Evie would have been mad over an unplanned trip to her doctor, she was going to go into orbit if we suggested a visit to the ER.

"I don't think we have a choice," I told Austin. "We're going to have to take her to the ER."

I had dialed nine and one when a loud thump from upstairs rattled the whole house. Both of us were out of our seats, bolting up the stairs without any thought.

I reached the top of the stairs first and came face to face with Evie who was struggling to walk down the hallway.

Swaying on her feet, she trailed one hand along the wall to steady herself as she tried to make it back to her bedroom from the bathroom.

"Evie, are you okay?" I took another step closer to her.

Hearing my voice, she turned drunkenly around to face me, and what I saw made me stop in the middle of the hallway.

Her eyes were glazed over and unfocused. Her gaze was moving around wildly, not able to focus on one place. A thin trail of blood was leaking from the corner of her left eye, and more blood covered her lips and smeared across one cheek.

"I threw up." Her voice was raspy, nearly unrecognizable, and she sounded detached, as if she wasn't really able to comprehend our conversation.

THREE
DAY 2

"Evie!" Alarmed, I stood rooted to the spot as I watched my friend sway sickeningly on her feet while her face was smeared with blood.

"What happened?" From behind me, Austin came forward and reached for his girlfriend. I'd forgotten for a second that he was back there.

Just as Austin reached her side, Evie's eyes rolled back into her head and she began to convulse violently.

"Evie!" he yelled as he dropped next to her, trying unsuccessfully to support her jerking limbs.

Still frozen, I watched a dark puddle grow under her twitching body.

"Call for help!"

The order jolted me back to awareness. I bolted back down to the living room where my phone lay when I dropped it just a minute ago. Fumbling with it, I punched the bottom button. My earlier aborted attempt to call for help lit up the screen, and I pushed the final number as I turned and ran for the stairs.

In my panic, I almost couldn't comprehend the drone of the busy signal.

"They're not answering!" I dropped to my knees next to my seizing friend.

Austin had rolled her to her side and was doing his best to support her head. The pungent smell of urine hit my nose at the same time I noticed the warmth seeping into my jeans.

"Try again!"

My shaking hands botched the job. Too many nines.

Hyperventilating, I tried again.

The drone of the busy signal was loud in the sudden silence of the hall. Evie had fallen utterly still and her limbs all fell limply to the floor. The only sounds were my harsh breathing and the frustrating buzz from the phone.

"Evie?" Austin gently rolled her onto her back. "Evie, can you hear me?"

I looked at the chalky complexion of my friend. Her eyes were closed and the streak of blood that had come from her eye had smeared all over her jaw line while red tinged froth dribbled from her slack mouth.

"She's too still," I said the last observation out loud as I leaned in closer to her chest.

"Evie?" With his voice reduced to a near whisper, Austin leaned over her face. Then turning his face toward me, he placed his ear close to her nose.

I watched as his already wide eyes filled with horror.

"I don't think she's breathing."

"What!" It came out as a shriek. Grabbing one of Evie's limp hands, I felt her wrist, looking for a pulse, but I couldn't find one. "No. No. No. No," I chanted under my breath as I dialed the phone again.

Screaming in frustration, I threw the useless phone away from me and even from the far end of the hall, the busy signal mocked me.

"We need to give her CPR."

Austin looked shell-shocked as he lightly patted Evie's bloodstained face, but hearing my suggestion, he nodded determinedly and tilted her head into what I hoped was the right position.

It had been a few years since my obligatory high school first aid class, and I prayed silently that I remembered it correctly as I clambered into position. I waited for Austin to pinch her nose and blow into her mouth before starting compressions.

Beneath my hands, her body still felt alarmingly hot.

Somewhere in my fourth set of compressions, I felt the sickening crack of a rib giving way under the force of my hands. Bile rose up the back of my throat, but I forced it back. I didn't have time for any of that now. Clinging to the faint memory of the first aid instructor telling the class that broken ribs were to be expected when giving CPR and hoping that it meant that I was doing this right, I kept going. I kept going until sweat dripped into my eyes and my arms burned with effort. I kept going even when sobs started to steal my breath.

My quivering arms were verging on collapse when I saw the glimmer of hope that I had been searching for. In my peripheral vision, I saw one of Evie's fingers twitch.

"There!" I gasped at Austin, who turned his grim gaze in the direction I was looking. I knew the moment he saw it too because an incredulous grin spread across his face.

"Evie, can you hear me?"

We watched as the finger twitched again, followed by the flexing of her whole hand.

"Evie?" Leaning down, Austin pressed his ear close to her nose again. "I still can't tell if she's breathing." He looked at me with a question in his brown eyes.

Any doubt that we had seen her hand move was erased when Evie's limbs all began to slowly come to life. She drew one leg up as her arms searched along the floor until her hand connected with Austin's.

Folding her hand in both of his, Austin stayed close to whisper, "Evie, it's okay. Bri and I are both here."

Evie's eyes suddenly snapped open, and I sucked back a gasp. They were completely bloodshot to the point that the whites had been taken over completely by bright red. She rolled her eyes before focusing on Austin, who was hovering over her. Struggling to sit upright, she tugged at the hand that was in his grasp while her eyes focused on his face with an intensity that sent a tendril of unease down my spine.

"Evie, maybe you shouldn't sit up yet. I think you might have a broken rib." I tried to convince her to stay down, but she gave no indication that she heard what I just said.

Her mouth worked but no sounds came out.

Straining to lean closer to Austin, she finally managed to lever herself higher on her arms that didn't quite want to work. Her lips moved again.

"What is it?" Austin leaned down to get his ear closer to her mouth.

Watching the exchange from less than two feet away, a flicker of unease bloomed inside me. The intensity of her gaze that was locked onto his face, plus the workings of her mouth that were starting to look less like an attempt at talking, reminded me of a dog eyeing a tasty bone.

"Austin." A warning tone escaped me. "Something is wrong."

He flicked his eyes in my direction, and at the moment he was focused on me, Evie made one final lunge. I watched in horror as she sank her teeth that were already stained with traces of her own blood into her boyfriend's face.

Yelping, I shot to my feet as Austin yelled out at the sudden pain. Then he shoved Evie back to the floor and stood up.

"What are you doing?" He looked at his blood stained hand that he used to swipe across his wound.

Still staring with that predatory look in her eyes, Evie scrambled to her feet with none of her usual grace, and without hesitation, she launched herself at Austin. In the confined space of the hallway, he had nowhere to escape her attack. Evie crashed into Austin, biting into the arm that he had tried to hold up in front of him.

Growling an animalistic sound that should never have come from a human throat, she released her bite on his arm. She clung in front of him and dragged herself closer as he tried to shove her away from his body. Evie proved impossible to dislodge and when Austin shoved her broken ribs, she didn't seem to notice what should have been extreme pain as she brought her teeth close to her goal.

Unable to react—either to help Austin or to run—I watched in shock as Evie bit deeply into her boyfriend's neck. In a trance, I watched the horrific amount of blood that immediately covered both of their fronts.

Austin sank to the floor under the ferocity of her attack and before long, Evie was crouched over his unmoving body.

Guttural growls broke the silence.

Putting one foot behind the other, I started backing away from the scene at the end of the hall, but when my foot found the creaky floorboard, I froze. Hearing the noise, Evie stopped whatever she was doing and went still for a moment. Then she slowly turned her body so she could see me standing frozen down the hall. She cocked her head slightly to the side and watched me with dead eyes.

Afraid to move for fear of provoking an attack, I stayed perfectly still.

Evie stared at me for the longest seconds of my life before opening her mouth and screaming a scream that raised every hair on my body.

Bolting toward the nearest door, I catapulted myself into the bathroom. The room was not all that large and offered no escape route, but at that point, all I wished for was a closed door in between myself and the creature that Evie had become.

Hitting the tiled floor, my feet slipped in something slick and I crashed to my hands and knees. Flipping over, the red of Evie's eyes blazed at me from just a foot away. Her mouth was open wide in mid scream and blood-stained spit flew out of it. Reacting on instinct, I kicked the door shut just in time for Evie to crash headlong into it.

Scrambling around, I slammed up against the door, simultaneously reaching to turn the lock.

If you enjoyed this sample, look for
The First 30 Days
on Amazon.

PETER OKAFOR

LIBERATION
REMNANTS OF MEN SERIES

CHAPTER ONE
Runner of Rat Town

There were no clouds in the sky, nothing but a grey mass stretching to ends unknown. The last yellow sunshine was seen twenty years ago. He was not born then, but everyone knew the tales of those wonderful rays that would kiss a skin with great warmth.

Those days were memories to some and nothing but a myth to others like Runner. He did not care much for a large ball of fire. All he wanted was to join the well-paid guards of Section 5, and that was the reason he was standing before the first dead body he had seen since birth.

He stood motionless and squeezed his face, covering his nose with his hands to keep the obnoxious smell away. It was the body of an elderly woman half burnt by a fierce radioactive storm that swept beyond the domed comforts of MegaCityOne at an hour interval. A silver handgun sat on the palm of her right hand, and resting on her body was a dead baby with a bullet hole in his head. There wasn't much investigation to the horrid scene as all connections seemed to be in place.

Runner felt a blunt pain in his heart. He knew that was very much a fate destined for half the poor folks that lived outside the protective dome of MegaCityOne.

His best friend, Troy Decker, hissed. "Come on, Runner. She suffered a better fate than any of us would hope."

Runner tightened the belt that held his gears around his waist. It was hard to be brave when the entire world wanted a piece of him. It was even harder to survive a world where air and water could cost a man his life savings. No thanks to Reinhardt Reddit, the tyrant that left half the planet at the mercy of radiation.

He raised his hand and gazed at an old wristwatch that had all its silver coating worn out by time, but it still displayed time accurately.

"10:30 AM. Oh my god!" He raised his gaze to the sky. "Oh my god! We have less than five minutes. Move, everyone, move."

Dust grew in the air like fumes from an exhaust. He inhaled the air, the sour taste unwelcomed on his tongue. He curved his hands over his brow and looked further. In the distance, a large storm of dust was raging forward. Runner turned around to see how many were behind. He waved his hand and shouted at the top of his voice, signaling a crowd of wayfarers to hasten.

Troy grasped an end of his torn beige jacket. "We've gotta go, man. We-got-to-go." He stressed the last words.

"Where is the cargo?" Runner asked, but Troy gave no answer.

Runner seized him by the neck of his jacket. "Troy, where is the cargo?"

"I don't know…I kinda left it behind. You know, the storm and all that shit made me panic." Troy looked woeful.

"What do you mean you left it behind? That's our ticket to never going hungry again, our ticket to Section 5 and then to the comforts of MegaCityOne—the paradise in this damned wasteland. You know there are people in that truck. Human beings, Troy…human beings."

Runner took another look at the raging storm. It was like the waves of a restless sea, one of those in the tales of Old Max—his colony's mad mechanic. The old man had told him once that the storms were poisonous radiation that could melt a skin in seconds. He didn't know how true that was, but the melting part of the story—that was definitely certain.

"Give me your cloak." He stretched his arm towards Troy.

Troy pulled his long black cloak and handed it to Runner. "What do you want with it?"

"Just get the others to safety." Runner threw the cloak on and made sure no part of his body was exposed.

He used a dusty turban to wrap his head and then put on dark goggles to protect his vivid brown eyes.

"Are you crazy, Runner? I know for certain you don't have any more stash of Sense pills left. You won't last a heartbeat out there," Troy spoke sternly.

"Just go. I will see you in five."

Runner paused for a moment and inhaled deeply. He ran into the growing storm of hot fog and dust. His feet sank into scattered scraps of bricks and metals as he struggled to push forward. The heat was becoming unbearable, and it stung his flesh with a burning sensation. His goggles protected his eyes, but he could barely see the cargo truck that was a few steps away from him.

He managed through the sinking scraps and reached the window of the truck. Everything was covered by dust. He used his hand to wipe the dust off the window and peeped. There were men, women, and children clustered together at one end, awaiting nature's wrath. Runner slammed his fist on the window, and a man wounded it down.

"What happened?"

"We can't get our truck to move. We are all going to die here!" the man screamed in confusion.

"Calm down." Runner urged. "How many do you carry?"

"Roughly forty," the man answered hysterically.

"Okay…okay." Runner opened the door and pulled the man down from the truck. "You see that storm in the distance?"

The man nodded.

"It will be here in two minutes. Gather everyone together. We can make it to the city gate before that storm hits us. Can you do that?"

The man nodded again and turned around, calling everyone out. They were all a bunch of the big city inhabitants, who—for some reason—had gone out of the city. They knew nothing of life outside the comforts of MegaCityOne. Well, it seemed nature had a lesson to teach.

Runner had survived by guiding passengers through the ruins of the barren waste beyond his home. It paid enough to keep him fed. Before, he never did care. Wealthy folks meant big bucks for him, and that was all that really mattered. But staring at their faces, his heart would never free him from torment if he abandoned them to die.

"Move! Move!" Runner bellowed.

The passengers rushed down the vehicles. They moved like a herd in a stampede, running towards the towering gate of the city. Runner felt the discomfort on his skin grow intense. The storm would hit them soon. He could feel it. He needed to push them to press forward with haste, or they will all die horrible deaths.

With each stride, the gates of MegaCityOne grew closer. Troy had already made it into the city with a few others that had left earlier, and he beckoned at Runner to move faster.

A loud thud sounded. Runner stopped and turned quickly to see an elderly man who had stumbled into a pile of rubble. The poor man's right foot was caught in blocks of broken concrete. That moment, Runner's mind was conflicted. He had two choices: help the man and get obliterated or continue onwards to the safety of the domed city.

In a quick decision, he took a step forward. Runner leaned towards him and stretched his hand to reach for the man. The storm was mere inches away.

"Give me your hand," Runner yelled.

The words had barely left his mouth when he found himself dragged backwards by an unknown person.

"Let him go, Runner. You can't help him." He heard Troy's voice.

Troy pulled him through the gate. The storm engulfed the man, melting his flesh quickly into flakes of red-hot ash.

The enormous metal gate slammed shut to prevent the storm from passing through.

Runner sank to the ground on both knees and hung his head in disappointment. People die all the time—he knew that—and the fact that mortality rates have really surged was not a fictional account. For some reason, the death of the man seemed to weigh heavy on his heart.

A hand came upon his shoulder. "I don't understand why you feel this need to save everyone in trouble. It is not your fault that a man cannot walk outside the dome without his gas mask. It is not your fault that the skies can only manage acid rains. These folks knew the cost of surviving in this world before they set out."

"Perhaps they shouldn't have." Runner stood to his feet. "A man risks his life on promises of better days for what? To ensure that his children endure a life of shit and piss? Look around you, Troy. Things can never get better than this. A man would have a better time choosing to ingest poison than living in this sewer pit we call home."

Troy put his arm over Runner's shoulder. "It is the life we find ourselves in, my friend. Come, let's go get our pay from the chief enforcer."

Finally, something good that could come out of all the despair he had endured. That pay was the light at the end of a tunnel. He could literally hear his rumbling stomach, how deeply it cried for sustenance.

Runner trailed behind his friend as they ascended the stairs of a towering outpost that overlooked the gates of Rat Town. The slum town was his home and one among ten colonies that had become the slums of MegaCityOne. The lingering smile on Troy's face only proved one thing to be true—the mere thought of a full belly could make a slum dweller happy for weeks. But truth be told, Troy wasn't the only one that bore that joy. Runner was no different; he was only good at concealing his enthusiasm.

"Guys, guys, guyssss…" a voice called from behind.

Runner missed a step and almost stumbled as he heard that voice. In the entirety of Rat Town and even the MegaCityOne itself, only one person made him so tense—Dope "Skittish" Davies. Nothing good ever came from associating with Dope, literally. He was an only child to the chief enforcer, an ideal role model to any aspiring psychopath.

"Here we go," Troy muttered without turning to look behind.

Runner turned around to face Dope. "What do you want, Skittish?" He had said that, having a good idea what was about to come.

"My father asked me to take care of…whatever it is he asked of you," Dope said, waving his arm incessantly.

Unlike Runner who was of average height and lean build, Dope was a short, burly boy, thickly muscular with powerful shoulders that could intimidate anyone. But Runner knew within all that sinew was a pathetic excuse for a boy who found pleasure in mockery and guile.

"Where is the cargo?" Dope asked, looking around.

Runner knew this was coming. He grimaced at the thought of something far worse. "We…" He glanced at Troy. "I didn't come with the cargo. I ran into a bit of a situation, and I chose to secure the passengers first."

"Oooh!" Dope raised his gaze to the sky putting his hands on his waist. "You're so not getting paid today."

CHAPTER TWO
Fight or Flight

"Damn you, Dope!"

Runner surged forward with both hands curled into a fist.

Troy got to him quickly. He threw his arms around Runner's torso to hold him back. Good thing he did. Three boys and a girl descended the stairs of the outpost and stood behind Dope. They bore fierce expressions and were all dressed in the black military garb of Section 5.

"Calm down, Runner," Troy whispered to him. "Or we would both leave here with one eye and empty pockets."

Dope's strength was the tons of hungry boys and girls who followed him around like the betas of a dog pack. He had bought their allegiances by securing a place for them amongst the well-paid guards of Section 5.

For any inhabitant of the slums, a job at Section 5 was reason enough to sell one's loyalty. It wasn't just about the pay, but the constant exploration of the wastelands provided opportunities to loot copper and other valuable scrap metals.

There was no need to press further. Runner's effort had been stretched thin chasing the dream that was Section 5. Now, as he stood before Dope's gang, he knew the only thing to do was to retreat with any little dignity he had left. Retreating meant another night spent twisting and turning on his hard bed and listening to the rumbling cries of his stomach.

His hunger he could manage, but how was he going to endure the cries of the two kids that had made him an underage guardian? They had been left to him by his deceased aunt. Desperate for a hot night meal, she had gone into the government's reserved hunting ground for a buck, but instead took a bullet from the guards. Her burden was now his, and as he lingered before Dope, those thoughts couldn't have hurt any worse.

Runner's fist trembled as he stared angrily at Dope. The best course of action was to turn around and leave. Dope would see it as a weakness and jump on every opportunity to cause him misery.

Dope raised his right hand. "Is this what you want?" He opened his palm and set loose tens of credit-chips to fall at his feet.

All that money falling to the ground, it made Runner's stomach churn at Dope's folly. He wanted the credits. They were his deserved pay for the day. But a gang of teenage boys and girls was the only thing keeping him from tearing Dope apart. Even if, somehow, he managed to get through them, Dope's dad was the chief enforcer of Section 5. The man would have the guards hang and cane him till his flesh peeled off.

"Come on, Runner." Troy pulled one end of his jacket to draw him back. "Let's go pick some scrap metal and sell to Old Max. We could at least get five credits for that, enough for two meals."

Troy and Runner turned away from Dope and began to walk away.

"Are you going to cry, Runner? Are you going to cry for Mommy and Daddy? Oh! I forgot. They have been rotting somewhere in the wastelands for years."

Dope burst into a loud laughter, expecting his gang to join, but it seemed they didn't share his enthusiasm and left him to an embarrassing lonely laughter.

Runner tensed and tried to turn, but Troy grabbed his arm. "He is not worth your time. Leave him to his foolishness."

Troy was not one of the smartest or brightest boys in Rat Town, but he was the best soul Runner has ever known. He was kind and easy going, with a slow reaction to anger and his gentle blue eyes held his attributes in keen.

Both boys made their way towards the gates. In the distance, a large shadow was growing. Runner turned around, and despite having seen it many times, it still managed to amaze him every time. The shadow was cast by the stark walls of the big city, MegaCityOne. A bright artificial glowing light that had replaced the sun, slowly dimmed to give way to a silvery light, a perfect replica of the moon's beam.

He had never seen the sun or moon, nor basked beneath their glorious beams. But he wished it every day, more than he wished for improved living conditions in Rat Town, his home.

For a moment, he stood still and imagined how life in the MegaCityOne would be like. He wished himself in the shoes of one of its wealthy residents or a son of an elite government official. Those folks had everything despite the limited resources available to mankind growing thinner by the day.

A loud horn bellowed. Guards from Section 5 drew the mighty gates open, and several armoured cars drove in, raising dust in the air. The cars were new designs by the Citadel of Engineering in MegaCityOne to navigate through the radiated wastelands, or so he had been told by Old Max the mechanic.

"I heard that the cost of water has risen in MegaCityOne," Troy whispered to Runner as they stared at the armed men of Section 5 unloading equipment from the vehicles. "Dictator Patterson tasked Section 5 with the job of finding a freshwater lake."

"Come on, Troy. Have you been listening to Old Max's crazy stories again? He is a good source of information, but if you get too comfortable, he will feed you false hopes of paradise and mountains with streams of honey," Runner said.

"It's true," Troy retorted. "They are running short of water in the big city. They said the dams have run dry and you can only get acid rains in the wastelands."

How is that my problem? Runner thought and then laughed softly. "If only they will all die of thirst so that we can go over there and loot their corpses."

"You can't mean that." Troy glanced at him.

"Speak for yourself," Runner answered.

He caught a glimpse of a girl he knew amongst the guards of Section 5. She was ebony-skinned with creamy cascading hair. Bag after bag, she unloaded the truck where she stood behind a gangly boy with a ridiculously small head and did not seem to notice Runner.

"Rhiannon!" he called.

She raised her head. "Runner." Her arm went up, waving at him.

Runner slung his makeshift axe across his back and held it tight with a belt that ran over his chest. He took quick strides to reach her.

"Is it true?" Runner's eyes were afire with curiosity.

"Is it true, what?" she asked.

"That Section 5 is searching for a fresh water lake?" He continued.

Rhiannon sat on the back of the truck. Her hair scattered on her shoulder, and it intrigued Runner the way they adhered to her movements. Troy joined soon enough and rested his back on the truck.

"It is true," she replied, much to Troy's delight.

"We are chasing after rumours and myths now. We scoured the wastelands, but there wasn't a single evidence of water. We even lost three boys in the process. There is something out there in the shadows of the building ruins. I could feel it—the rage. Something took those boys, Runner, but the chief enforcer would not listen. I shudder to think what might become of us all."

Rhiannon jumped down the truck and opened her arms to hug Runner who received the embrace warmly. She was his best friend too, despite Troy's nagging comments that she felt something more than that. He knew indeed that love and family was the only thing that kept most folks going in Rat Town, yet they were the hardest to come by.

"I need a favour," Runner spoke softly.

Rhiannon wiped her hands on a ragged cloth. "What is it?"

"We lost our pay because of a misunderstanding with Skittish, and now we need to get some scrap metal to sell to Old Max."

"In other words, you need to sneak into the wastelands." Rhiannon supported her hands on her waist. "But you know if I get caught opening any of the small gates for you guys, I will lose my job."

"Please, Rhee. If not for us, think about those kids at home. We can't let them cry through the night." Troy added, and Runner nodded.

"I got paid today, hundred credits in all. I can get something for your aunt's kids." She sunk her hand in a small bag hanging at her waist.

A hundred credits were enough to last a family for a month, but as much as he wanted a share of it, Runner knew Rhiannon's family needed every bit of the credits.

"Here, this is ten." She stretched her hand towards Runner.

He held her hand and closed her fingers on the credit-chips.

"Your mom is sick. Use it to take care of her. We won't implicate you if we get caught in the wastelands, I promise."

After a moment of consideration, Rhiannon sighed. "Fine, follow me," she said.

Both boys followed behind Rhiannon. Their strides were hastened yet careful not to alert a guard that stood high on a watchtower. The wiry man turned around a large watch light to check for trespassers. Rhiannon stopped, and the boys did the same, pressing their backs on the side of a car.

"Duck," she whispered, and they obeyed.

Squatting on his toes, Runner peered from the side of the car. Three guards from Section 5 were tearing out posters of a black skull with two daggers crossed over it.

"They are taking off posters of Death Throe," Runner whispered to his friends.

"Yes...yes...yes, now I remember. I heard the rebel was responsible for the water shortage. He sabotaged water reserve pipelines. Apparently, he was setting it free for the common folks. Didn't change a thing though. A gallon of water still goes for twenty credit-chips. That's twice what I make in a day...if I work hard."

"How did you know all this?" Runner asked.

"Old—"

"Max told me," they all said simultaneously.

"What?" Troy shared his gaze between them. "It's true."

The guards passed on, and Rhiannon stood to her feet. "Come on guys, over there." She pointed at an abandoned factory.

The three ran towards the building, quick enough to escape the watchtower's line of sight. Runner slammed his shoulder on the metal door, and it opened easily.

"Wow," he said as he entered, staring at a large television screen. "It's been long since I've seen one of these."

He scanned the gadget with his eyes, searching for a power button.

"Everything here is Section 5's property. Don't put me in further trouble by breaking anything, boys," Rhiannon said solemnly.

Runner found and hit the button. The screen came alive, displaying the image of a blonde girl standing behind a podium and surrounded by newsmen from the Citadel of Journalism.

Daughter of Supreme Councilor Peter Patterson has vowed to stand against the menace of the rebel, Death Throe. The government will, hereby, relocate all resources towards...

"That's Olivia Patterson." Rhiannon pointed at the screen.

Runner turned it off. "More like the princess of MegaCityOne. That girl is just my age, and she got the whole world wrapped under her fingers. She is real pretty. I bet she would make a decent babe."

"And what are you going to offer her, eh? Your tattered shoes or that bundle of iron rods you call a bed?" Troy chuckled. "Keep dreaming, my friend. We both know we are going to die long before the big city will be opened to any of the slum dwellers."

Rhiannon laughed at both boys and turned around to face a locker. She opened it and revealed a stash of tools.

"Over here, guys. You could use this as weapons. The wasteland is not where you want to be at night, unarmed."

Runner approached the locker and picked a wrench and a knife. He was quite good at fashioning makeshift weapons, and just seeing both tools, the image of an axe grew in his mind. Yet he couldn't still resist the thought of burying it on Dope's shoulder.

If you enjoyed this sample, look for
Liberation
on Amazon.

T.M. MENDES

INTERTWINED
BOUND SERIES
BOOK ONE

CHAPTER ONE

The sun beat down over me, making sweat drop onto my sticky pink tank top. I bent over in the back seat of my beat-up orange Gremlin, placing the last of my boxes inside. Swiping my blonde hair out of my face, I stood upright again and turned toward my parents. Mom, as usual, looked beautiful even with tears in her eyes; it made the blue in them pop out. My dad stood next to her like a strong pillar. His stone gray eyes that I had inherited softened at the sight of me.

"It's okay. I'll be back here for holidays before you know it," I said before wrapping my arms around the both of them. Mom hugged me back tight, almost too tight.

"I know. It's just my baby is headed off to college! I'm so proud of how you turned yourself around last year. Now, look where you are. You've been accepted to Arizona State University! You can call day or night, okay?" my mom said as she held my face. Chuckling at her antics, I nodded, or at least moved my head the best I could while she held my head captive.

"I know, Mom. I love you both, but if I'm going to get there by nightfall, I need to leave now." We lived in Tuba City, Arizona. It was a nearly four-hour drive to Phoenix, and

I had a late start. I was going to leave this morning with my one and only friend, Gavin, but I wanted to wait to say goodbye to my dad too since work kept him late. Gavin had gotten accepted to the same college. We were both pretty excited.

It's funny because before my junior year, we weren't really friends. In fact, I think he used to hate me. But one day, I said something that made him laugh. That was that, and now we're all but attached to the hip.

"Goodbye, Kiddo. Drive safe, and watch the needle so you won't overheat." My dad always talked about getting a better car, but I was living off a student income, which meant I had next to nothing in my bank. Pretty standard as far as college life goes. I was lucky to get a scholarship even though it did surprise me since there were other students that were more qualified. I was told the reason was I volunteered quite a bit these last two years.

Saying goodbye one more time, I hopped into my car and sped off to my future.

* * *

I stood outside of the campus with my mouth agape at its size. Students walked up and down the designated sidewalks, not too bothered by the blistering heat. I had to stop twice on the way here so my car didn't overheat, and I was pretty sure a few of my CDs melted in the back seat since it smelled like burnt plastic. I had texted Gavin a while ago that I was thirty minutes out, so when I saw him walking up, I wasn't surprised. He grinned when he saw me, showing off his green braces. His wire-rimmed glasses glinted in the setting sun, making me squint my eyes. Without warning, he picked me up and spun me around in three quick circles. When he set me down, I had to look up since he was significantly taller than me.

"Hey, Miss Always Late!" He teased and picked up a box that I had set outside of the car. I was right about some of my CDs. They might as well be used for some sort of abstract art for all the good they were now. I playfully scowled at him before picking up my duffel bag and swinging it over my shoulder and picking up another box. I had one more on the ground, so after a second, I placed the box in my hands down and placed the smaller one on top of it and picked them both up. I was determined to make it just one trip.

"Thanks for the help. I guess I'm in dorm 118. Do you know where that is?" I asked, huffing a bit at the big load I was carrying. I laughed tiredly as Gavin scooped the top box out of my arms and onto his box. "Thanks," I said distractedly.

"No problem, and yeah, I know where it is. Just across the courtyard where I'm staying at. Do you have a roommate?" He huffed alongside me. I nodded, still taking in all the sites around me.

"Yeah, but she's not going to be here until the end of the month. At least that's what my paper says. Who's your roommate?" I swear I could feel myself baking as the sweat on my forehead sizzled.

"His name is Hayden. You might meet him later, but I'd give him a wide berth if I were you." The warning in his voice rung clear. I gave him a puzzled look.

"Why?" I asked, perplexed. Gavin, although he looked a little nerdy, wasn't known to stand down.

"He's bad news. In the minutes that I've met him, I got that vibe from him. He smelled like pot and has a bad attitude." I felt bad Gavin had to be stuck with a roommate like that. I hoped mine wasn't like that.

"Hopefully, it will get better. And if not, I think you can switch if someone is willing." I tried to be helpful, but at hearing him snort in disagreement, I knew I wasn't.

"That's the problem! Anyone I talked to today told me to stay away from him. No one likes him! And when you're near him, you get this weird feeling like you need to stay away." I felt a little offended that he would say that since I went through a similar thing growing up.

"Maybe he's like me? Everyone tried to stay away from me growing up." Before I could say anything else, he snorted out a loud laugh.

"No way! You were little miss popular growing up!" We always argued on how my childhood was. I distinctly remembered being alone a lot in school, but who knows since it was so long ago.

"Whatever, can we please just head inside where hopefully it's air-conditioned before I become buzzard food?" I complained as sweat started to sting my eyes. I was sure I looked really attractive.

"You got it. We just need to go through this building here." Gavin directed us into a building that thankfully had an AC on.

* * *

"Do you think you can get me some numbers while you're living here?" Gavin spoke as another cute girl walked past. I shook my head and chuckled.

"Oh no! We are not going down that road again! Last time I tried to set you up, Amanda didn't speak to me for a month!" I laughed as we reached my dorm room door. I had to set the box and bag down to fish the key out of my pocket in my jean shorts before I could open the door. My classmate Amanda was a cute shy girl. Gavin still didn't realize why taking her to see a museum that had a spider collection was such a bad idea.

When we walked in, a smile lit up my face. It was small, but it was mine. Two beds on opposite sides of the room were no bigger than a twin but still looked comfy. A desk laid under the two tall beds like a little cove, and I could see the engravings on the wood from where I stood that came from past students. There was only one fairly large closet near the door with a large bay window on the far wall looking out into the campus. Overall, it looked like freedom, and I could feel my heart racing at all the new possibilities. "I felt the same way seeing my dorm for the first time this morning," Gavin said after seeing I was speechless.

"It feels great…C'mon, let's set these down, then I want to explore." Gavin nodded, and I quickly chose my bed by the far wall. I wasn't sure how loud my roommate would be, but I knew I had quiet footsteps so I wouldn't wake her when I came in late, which was why I chose the farthest bed. Gavin placed my boxes on my bed before we walked out. Locking the door behind me, I placed the key back into my jeans pocket and smiled up at Gavin. "Show me around!" I ordered playfully. He laughed through his nose, shaking his head before gesturing me to follow him.

The common area was amazing! A lot of the walls were glass so you could see outside, while the solid walls were white and had a chic designer feel. Colorful couches splashed personality to the open area while lighting fixtures gave the room a warm feel. Paintings that littered the walls also gave off that quirky vibe, but it meshed well with everything.

"This place is amazing! I can tell I'm going to like it here," I spoke with a smile. Students were either messing around or studying dutifully in a quiet corner. Gavin nudged my shoulder for me to continue to follow him.

"I believe the cafeteria is this way. Follow me because I'm starving," he said while rubbing his stomach. I rolled my eyes at him since he was almost always hungry. It really wasn't fair since he could eat an entire pizza by himself and not gain an ounce.

"I doubt it, but I'm hungry too. Have you had the food here yet? Is it any good?" I asked, watching my steps so I didn't bump into anyone. Suddenly, a horde of students brushed past us, and all I got from the murmuring is the word *fight*. Gavin and I paused before he stopped a guy who was running.

"Hey, what's going on?" he asked quickly.

"That guy Hayden again." The unnamed guy took off after that. Gavin paled slightly and shook his head before taking my arm and towing the both of us in the opposite direction. I had to nearly run to keep up since his legs were so much longer than mine. Puffing slightly as we got outside, I pulled out from his grip.

"Can you slow down?" I asked with slightly labored breath. The heat was like a smack in my face, like a living breathing thing that was suffocating me. Gavin wouldn't listen though, so I had to run slightly ahead and stand in front of him. "Can you stop?" I asked exasperatedly.

"What?" He huffed. "Can't I be a little peeved that my roommate whom I've only met once is in another fight? Why did I have to get stuck with the campus bad guy?" I had to bite my lip to stop the threatening smile coming over my face.

"Peeved?" I clarified with a slight snicker. I saw a faint blush take over his cheeks, but he shook it away.

"Well, I am! What if this guy decides to kill me in my sleep? Then what?"

I rolled my eyes at him and shook my head. "I'd miss you terribly," I spoke with a mock pout. He pushed my shoulder some before he started walking again, this time at a more reasonable pace.

"I'm serious though! You know me. I'm not one to just back down, but it doesn't mean I go looking for trouble."

I got where he was coming from, but I think he'll be fine. "You shouldn't worry too much. You'll be okay if you just stay out of each other's way. I know it will be hard since you're basically living with one another, but it will work out. You'll see."

He sighed and reluctantly nodded. I heard a rumbling, sound making me look down at Gavin's stomach. I laughed and poked him before stepping away. "I think we should feed the beast before it consumes everyone in its path." I joked.

"Hardy har har." The sarcasm in his voice was thick and made me laugh. After a few more minutes, we were able to find the cafeteria and grab something to eat. I got a fruit salad and a bottle of tea while Gavin opted out for a huge burger.

"So what's your schedule?" I asked with my mouth full of grapes. Gavin shot me a disgusted look playfully before throwing a napkin my way.

"First off...close your mouth, and secondly, I have Math and Science on Wednesdays and Thursdays in the morning while English and Photography are on Mondays and Fridays in the evening. What about you?" he asked, still inhaling his burger.

"And you think I'm disgusting?" I asked, eying the large amount of mustard on his chin before throwing the napkin his way. "I have English and Art Mondays and Tuesdays in the afternoon, while I have Literature 101 and Math 102 Thursdays and Saturdays in the morning. Man, we'll have, like, no classes together! How am I supposed to survive?" I asked, sulking into my fruit. I felt Gavin pat my back awkwardly before clearing his throat.

"You could always make new friends? Besides, we'll see each other on the weekends." I rolled my eyes at the idea. He knew I wasn't great at making friends but stayed silent anyways. I didn't feel like arguing over something as small as that. Sitting back against my seat, my eyes drifted around the large and loud room. Mindless chatter provided a void to fill the silence in my mind, but as I sat there letting my gaze drift from one student to the other, I began to feel the small tug on my heart missing my parents. I tried to shake it off, but it persisted. After all, this was the first time I would be away from them. My eyes shot to Gavin as he placed his hand over mine in comfort.

"I'm fine." I lied, wanting to be stronger than I felt. What kind of an eighteen-year-old can't make it a day without missing her parents? I felt like a little girl again, and I didn't like it. Pulling my hand back from under his, I looked elsewhere knowing if he really pushed, I would spill everything. I heard him sigh, but he didn't say anything else. Instead, we both sat quietly observing our fellow peers thinking to ourselves.

* * *

"Thanks for helping me out today," I said with a grin, looking up at Gavin. He shrugged carelessly and pushed up his glasses since they were perched on the tip of his nose. We were standing outside my door room as fatigue and tiredness washed over me. I could hear the call my bed was singing to me, making my hand twitch to fling open the door and answer.

"No problem. Oh, I almost forgot! I got you something." Gavin dug into the pocket of his jeans before pulling out a whistle on a rope. I quirked an eyebrow in question.

"A whistle?" I asked, a little perplexed. It was a little strange. It's not everyday someone gives you a whistle. Gavin shook his head and sighed.

"It's for your safety. I kind of figured we wouldn't get to see a whole lot of each other like normal, so I got you this. If you get into trouble, blow it so it will scare off anyone who's trying to hurt you," he explained, making that imaginary light bulb go off above my head.

"Ah, okay. Thanks, Gavin!" I took the whistle and wrapped the rope around my wrist a few times to keep it there. I saw his ears turn red from my gratitude, making me chuckle. I patted his arm and said, "Good night. I'll see you tomorrow, okay?"

He nodded, giving me the 'go ahead and head off to bed' signal. I turned and opened my door before shutting it behind me. It was eerily quiet in my room, causing the slight loneliness to seep back in. I had this feeling in the pit of my stomach that something was off, but doing a quick survey of my room, nothing seemed different. Shrugging it off, I got out my cell phone to check the time. I saw a text from my mom.

Love you, sweetie. Be safe and call us tomorrow after you're settled in.

Part of me wanted to call now just to talk, but I bit back the pressure building behind my eyes and got undressed instead. I had to start acting like an adult, and calling my parents within hours of seeing them because I was homesick didn't exactly scream 'adult.' Pulling on an oversized sweatshirt, I untucked my blonde hair and settled in bed before drifting quickly to sleep.

* * *

"*Run...faster!*" A voice echoed like the wind that whipped around me. I knew I was scared, but not why. In fact, I was downright terrified as I gasped for air. My eyes squinted, trying to find where the voice was coming from, but all I saw was an empty street.

"*Run!*" it yelled again, making me whimper. I felt helpless tears threaten to spill as I choke.

"Where?" I screamed, knowing this voice was trying to help me, but I could feel the hairs on the back of my neck stand straight. They were coming for me. Who? I didn't know, but I knew they were bad...very bad. Suddenly, I saw a movement on the far street corner. A man with black hair stood under a desolate street lamp. The shadow marred his face so I couldn't see who it was, but I knew he was the source of the voice. My feet felt like lead, but I pushed harder to run toward him. I was struggling while he stood there waiting. Why wouldn't he help me?

I screamed when cold, claw-like hands wrapped around my torso as I was halfway there. It was pulling me away from the stranger. They were too strong! I couldn't break away! "Help!" I screamed so loud my throat felt raw. I was getting farther and farther away from the man on the corner. I could feel through the hands that grabbed me that with them came certain death.

"Not fast enough..." I heard him just over the howling wind while I was being dragged back into the shadows.

* * *

"No!" I sprung up in a cold sweat. I could feel my head throbbing fiercely in time with my heartbeat. Stunned, my eyes saw it was just getting light outside. With my hands shaking, I wiped away the remaining sweat from my forehead and got up, knowing I couldn't fall back asleep after that. I was in shock. That was the first dream I had in years. I always thought it was odd I really never had dreams, and I'm not talking about the ones you can't remember, but I literally wouldn't dream of anything. It was always black, and tonight, I had one, and not just a dream but a nightmare. Something didn't settle right in my gut, but all I wanted right now was to shower off the grime I felt on my skin, and possibly wash away the images assaulting my mind.

 Grabbing a random white t-shirt and a pair of blue yoga pants, I also got the necessary bathroom needs such as towel and shampoo. When I quietly padded down the hallway barefoot, I noted it seemed ghostly. Not a soul in sight and the only sound that could be heard was the slight hum of the lights and the AC combined. My heart was still beating slightly above normal from the nightmare that I experienced while my palms were still clammy. Trying to shake it off, I sped up my walk at a brisk pace. My eyes jumped from wall to wall, thinking the creatures in my dream might possibly pop out suddenly. I felt relief wash over me when I made it to the public shower but had to laugh at myself for acting so paranoid. If anyone were awake now and saw my state, they'd think I was mad.

 I sighed deeply when the warm water cascaded onto my skin. My eyes closed as I could almost feel my tension melt away. I grabbed my coconut-scented shampoo and began the process of cleaning not only my body but my mind as well.

 "She's becoming immune…" A crackly almost nonexistent voice rung through the air. I gasped and turned around to face the curtain that blocked me from view. My heart was back up to full speed. With a shaky hand, I peeked from behind my barrier and let go of the breath I was holding.

 Another girl around the same age was on her phone as she brushed her hair, still in her pajamas. She felt my eyes on her, making her look up in the mirror to meet my gaze.

 "Oh! Sorry. Did I scare you? I thought you heard me come in…No, Jackie, not you; this girl who's in the shower."

I realized she now was tuned back into her previous conversation on the phone.

"It's okay. It just freaked me out for a second," I replied quickly and turned off the water in my shower before grabbing my towel that was hanging on a hook just outside the stall. Once I had wrapped myself securely, I stepped out and gave her a small smile. She grinned back through the mirror, showing off a perfect set of white teeth. She then stopped brushing her red curls and promptly told Jackie that she had to go and finish getting ready.

"Hi, again sorry for the scare, but my name is Jojo, but most people call me Joe." Her name fitted her as she seemed very chipper even this early in the morning. I took out my toothbrush with a friendly smile and looked at her through the mirror.

"Cali, and it's fine. I was just being a scaredy cat." Before I could stop myself and just brush my teeth, a question blurted past my lips. "What did you mean, 'She's becoming immune?'" I felt slightly mortified that I would ask a question that was *clearly* none of my business, but it was like my mouth filter went on the fritz. I quickly began to brush my teeth, hoping that would keep my mouth busy enough to not get me into any more trouble. I saw Joe cock her head in question.

"I never said anything like that," she answered before grabbing her stuff and leaving. While she could move perfectly, I was, however, more or less frozen. *If she never said that then...No, she could be lying. But why would someone lie about that?* I spat the excess toothpaste into the sink and rinsed my mouth out, inwardly cursing myself.

"Get a hold of yourself," I grumbled out and proceeded to get dressed. After I was done, I decided to go back to my dorm to really unpack my things. My fingers combed lazily through my hair since I left my hairbrush in my room. Unthinkingly, I paused outside my dorm room thinking something was lurking behind the door.

    I nearly wanted to hit myself for being childish.

    Groaning under my breath, I flung the door open after I unlocked it, but quickly flicked the light on. My eyes swept over everything. I was satisfied when nothing seemed out of place. Unconsciously, my hands were balled into fists, prepared to fight if the need showed itself. The glint that came off one of my bracelets caught my attention, making my eyes look for the source of light since I knew my ceiling light wouldn't be bright enough to do that.

    It was then I noticed that the sun had really started to rise above the large city. Bright colors were blended into a mixture of brilliant oranges, reds, and yellows. The sight stole my breath and reminded me of home. On the rare occasions I was up before the sun back home, I loved to sit outside and watch it come up from the valley hills. The painting nature was working before my eyes gave me the comfort I needed at the moment.

    It must have been another five or so minutes before the colors dulled into a sky blue. I sighed before going back to unpacking. I was sure Gavin wouldn't be up for another four to five hours since it was still extremely early. I bent over to retrieve my iPod dock and pushed play on a random song before getting to work.

    This was going to be a long day.

If you enjoyed this sample then look for
Intertwined: A Sci-Fi Romance Novel
on Amazon!

ACKNOWLEDGEMENTS

A big thank you to the many Wattpad friends who have supported these stories. Your kind words and encouragement have kept me going through a tough year.

AUTHOR'S NOTE

Thank you so much for reading *Luna*! I can't express how grateful I am for reading something that was once just a thought inside my head.

Please feel free to send me an email. Just know that my publisher filters these emails. Good news is always welcome.
lora_powell@awesomeauthors.org

I'd love to hear your thoughts on the book. Please leave a review on Amazon or Goodreads because I just love reading your comments and getting to know you!

Can't wait to hear from you!

Lora Powell

ABOUT THE AUTHOR

    I am a thirty something mother to one amazing daughter, who continually challenges me to be better at everything I do. Our family lives in the north east part of the US, but we love to travel and see new things.

    I have had a life-long love affair with books, but didn't work up the courage to try writing until about three years ago. After stumbling upon Wattpad, my addiction to creating these new little worlds grew. Hearing from my readers that one of my stories made them laugh, or cry, has become one of the highlights of my life. Reading can take you on an incredible journey, and if I can bring my readers even a small amount of happiness, then I consider my writing time well spent.

Made in the USA
Monee, IL
21 May 2024

58729628R00066